BEYOND THE GATES OF DREAM

BOOKS BY LIN CARTER

THE MAN WHO LOVED MARS
THE CITY OUTSIDE THE WORLD
LOST WORLDS
KESRICK
FOUND WANTING
THE TOWER OF MEDUSA
DESTINATION: SATURN
BEYOND THE GATES OF DREAM
KELLORY THE WARLOCK

The Chronicles of Kylix

THE QUEST OF KADJI
THE WIZARD OF ZAO

The Adventures of Thongor

THONGOR AND THE WIZARD OF LEMURIA
THONGOR AND THE DRAGON CITY
THONGOR AGAINST THE GODS
THONGOR IN THE CITY OF MAGICIANS
THONGOR AT THE END OF TIME

The Adventures of Eric Carstairs in Zanthodon

JOURNEY TO THE UNDERGROUND WORLD
HUROK OF THE STONE AGE
DARYA OF THE BRONZE AGE
ERIC OF ZANTHODON

The Gondwane Epic

THE WARRIOR OF WORLD'S END
THE ENCHANTRESS OF WORLD'S END
THE IMMORTAL OF WORLD'S END
THE BARBARIAN OF WORLD'S END
THE PIRATE OF WORLD'S END

Terra Magica

MANDRICARDO
CALLIPYGIA
DRAGONROUGE

BEYOND THE GATES OF DREAM

LIN CARTER

WILDSIDE PRESS
BERKELEY HEIGHTS, NJ • 1999

BEYOND THE GATES OF DREAM

Published by:

Wildside Press
P.O. Box 45
Gillette, NJ 07933-0045
www.wildsidepress.com

ISBN: 1-58715-078-6

BEYOND THE GATES OF DREAM
is dedicated to my agent,
HENRY MORRISON
who works hard trying to
sell my stories, and to the late
ANTHONY BOUCHER
who was the first editor to buy one.

CONTENTS

A Sort of Introduction, Called

HERE, AND BACK AGAIN

I AM an addict. I have a 164-page, Bok-covered, staple-fastened monkey on my back. And it's been there, more or less, since I was nine or ten or like that, way back before the Flood. . . .

When I was a kid, back in the middle of the 1930's, I was the sort of kid who thought it was more fun to poke around the back-corner shelves of the public library than to be out catching flies on second base (or whatever it is you *do* on second base). Now, I do not mean to put down those of you who would rather be out catching flies on second base: there isn't anything wrong with fly-catching: it just isn't my bag, that's all.

I had already eaten my way through the Oz books, Mary Poppins, *The Wind in the Willos*, Tom Swift, and the now-neglected works of a gentleman called Roy Rockwood. (. . . as you can see, the infection had already set in . . .) And I had (so I thought at

9

the time) exhausted all the nourishment there was to be found in Jules Verne—did you know, by the way, that his name isn't really supposed to be pronounced the way it looks to American readers, JOOLZ VERN? Nupe. Being as he's a Frog, it should be vocalized something like ZHOOL PHAIRN, more nor less. Sounds like wicked Jeddak . . .

Anyway, there I was prowling the shelves in search of succulent nutriment, half-deciding to go back and venture with *Ojo in Oz* once again . . . and I stumbled into a big fat shelf loading with plumpish books by some gink with the rather unlikely name of Edgar Rice Burroughs. Well, what the hell: I picked out one that looked fairly promising, checked it out at the big desk under the painting of Our Benefactor, Andrew Carnegie, and caught the streetcar home . . . and I can't honestly say that I remember much of what else happened that afternoon . . . I was too busy riding my trusty thoat across the dead sea-bottoms, my longsword slapping my naked thigh, the two moons hurtling through the void above, with stout old Tars Tarkas loping along at my side . . .

I was a goner from that moment on.

*

IT WAS great being a kid in the days when I was a kid. My folks lived in St. Petersburg, Florida: a medium-sized town, clean, sleepy, sunny, nice. Nothing much ever happened there. We lived on a quiet side-street off Tangerine Avenue; there weren't many kids around for me to play with, and the few who did live nearby were the type who preferred catching flies out on second base, so I just hung around the backyard most of the time, reading, playing with my dog Tip.

·To anyone watching me as a kid, it must have looked like the nether extremities of Dullsville. But it wasn't: I was having the time of my life; more excitement, more color, more magic, more thrills, more pure satisfaction was packed into those lazy, summery years than in the rest of my life rolled up in one big fat bundle of days. There was, literally, so much to do that there was hardly time enough to do it all. There were, of course, the drab necessities of life to be hurried through: school, homework, that sort of thing. But the rest of my time was one continuous voyage of discovery through the most enchanted worldful of wonders and perils ever set before a kid . . .

Here's how it was. Every afternoon after you got home from school there was the big Philco cabinet in the alcove between the dining room and the living room. You remained hunched over next to it for several enchanted hours, drinking in the fascinating adventures of Jack, Doc and Reggie on *I Love a Mystery* (and to this day I can draw a multithroated sigh of simultaneous nostalgia from a room of slightly balding businessmen in their forties, by pitching my voice to a high, nasal Texas accent and drawling, in imitation of the unforgettable Barton Yarborough, "Lookee here, son, honest to my grandma . . ."), and *Lights Outs* by Arch Oboler, and *Latitude: Zero*, to see if the Skipper and Simba, aboard the supersubmarine Omega, had yet penetrated the lava wall around the mystery isle to confront the villainous Madame Shark and recover the stolen idol of Kali . . .

Later in the afternoon, you might go down to the store around the corner to pick up some groceries for your mother, ostensibly. Actually, you wanted to

11

check the drugstore to see if the latest issue of Planet Comics was out yet, and to peek at the Big Little Books in McCrory's five-and-dime, hoping to find another just as good as *Maximo, the Amazing Superman* or of *Buck Rogers, 25th Century A.D., and the Overturned World* .·. .

But Saturday was really the Big Day of the week. You started out early in the morning; you went downtown to Red Ackerman's big newsstand and checked to make sure whether the latest issues of Startling Stories with that long-awaited new Leigh Brackett novel, *Sea-Kings of Mars,* was in yet . . . then you went down Central Avenue to your spiritual home, Haslam's second-hand book and magazine store. There was eighty-five cents burning a hole in your pocket, and no telling what might have turned up in the stacks of dog's-eared, dilapidated old pulps since last week . . . maybe another coveted issue of Doc Savage with *Seven Agate Devils* or *The Whisker of Hercules* in it . . . or another antediluvian copy of wonderful Weird Tales with yet another one of those enthralling Conan stories by Robert E. Howard . . . or a back issue of Famous Fantastic Mysteries, with a bewilderingly gorgeous Finlay cover, and A. Merritt's *The Snake Mother* therein . . .

Later, after a glorious hour of turning over heaps of mouldering pulps and getting your hands filthy, reeking with the delicious smell of book-dust, you went down to the Roxy Theatre to see Chapter Four ("Death Takes the Wheel") of *The Adventures of Captain Marvel,* to see if the big red cheese had finally gotten one of those dang lenses away from the sinister henchmen of The Scorpion yet. And, if you were lucky, the picture that played right after the serial might *not* be another dreary Roy Rogers in rust-and-blue Trucolor, but something scrumptious and yummy like Bela Lugosi and Lon Chaney, Jr., in *Frankenstein Meets the Wolfman*, with Patric Knowles and Ilona Massey . . .

And if the serial that week happened to be, as rarely was the case, something crummy like a Western, you could always skip the popcorn-redolent darkness of the Roxy and go down to The Playhouse two blocks away, where they might be reviving Errol Flynn in *Robin Hood*, with Olivia de Haviland as Maid Marian, Claude Rains as Prince John, Alan Hale as Little John and Eugene Palette as Friar Tuck . . . or way downtown to The Cameo, where Tyrone Power might be playing in *The Mark of Zorro*, with Basil Rathbone and Linda Darnell . . .

After the thrill-drenched adventures of Saturday, Sunday was always a bore. But at least there was the Sunday funnies you could count on, and a delicious hour spent over the gorgeous, richly colored full page of Alex Raymond art. You had been waiting all week to see how Flash Gordon made it over the snow-fields, and what happened when the flying snow-serpent attacked his party, and to find out if Count Malo was going to be as evil as he seemed, and to linger over another picture of lovely Queen Fria of Frigia with her blonde tresses braided and coiled to either side of her head, and to glom again her scantily clad beauty in that fascinating cellophane snow-suit . . .

With all this going on every week, week after week, who could possibly be bored? And what kind of a clunkhead wants to waste time catching flies on second base?

THOSE who are kids today have, honestly, no conception of how they have been gypped by not having been kids twenty-five years ago. What can they possibly do with their time? They have no movie serials to watch, no Big Little Books to read, no radio melodramas to listen to, no pulp magazines to devour all the way through to the letter-columns tucked amid *Ruptured? Throw Away That Smelly Old Truss!* ads. They have nothing much worthy of their attention in the Sunday funnies (with the lone exception of *Prince Valiant*, of course, for Hal Foster is still going strong, God bless 'im and preserve him at least till the age of 250!); and while there are still comic books around, the ones you get these days have been carefully sanitized, deodorized, and approved by the gimlet-eyed Comics Code. That means no nekkid wimmen tied up being whipped, and no nekkid wimmen strapped down to operating tables at the mercies of giggling fiends, no jolly gory torture or seduction episodes . . .

In fact, about the best there is these days is sleazy, also carefully de-juiced, television serials like *Lost in Space* or *Star Trek*, which are, believe me, pretty skimpy fare to feed growing young minds on.

All in all, and not that I wouldn't like to be ten or fifteen years younger, now that I find myself in the last couple of years before hitting the dreaded age of forty, I would not for any price have missed being a kid in the golden era when I *was* a kid. Thank God I had my mind thoroughly rotted with all that golden, priceless trash! Thank God my morals were wrecked, my ethics perverted, my taste forever tainted with a thirst for the gloriously fourth-rate! Thank God nobody worried about what loathsome effect all those junky comic books, movie serials, pulp magazines,

14

horror movies, and other magnificent garbage were doing to our tender young minds! Of *course* we all became sadistic young perverts, the whole starry-eyed, Lovecraft-loving, Shadow-collecting generation! And damn few of us would have had it any other way . . .

And (especially) I thank whatever Gods may be that during these tender, impressionable years of my youth I was carefully kept away from Good Books, Wholesome Literature, Deathless Poetry, Enduring Drama, and Approved Beloved Classics! That stuff can really rot the mind, folks, and I know whereof I speak, for I have met people whose entire childhoods were passed among Fine Literature, avoiding entirely the infectious Trash Syndrome: people who turn an unbelieving eye toward me when I frankly state that *I Love a Mystery* was the greatest show in the history of radio, that Rafael Sabatini can write rings around Jean Genet and Sartre and Camus, that *King Kong* is thirty times as great a movie as *Juliet of the Spirits* or *Blow-Up,* that there is more pure Magic for me in the single word "SHAZAM!" than in any given half-a-book by William Burroughs or thirty solid minutes of listening to Bob Dylan or Brahms.

Sure, there's nothing wrong with Literature, but for the love of all that's holy, you better come to it no earlier than your early twenties, or you can be ruined for life. During those golden years when my tastes were being permanently formed (or *de*formed, maybe), my mind permanently warped, and the horizons of my imagination permanently stretched to the boundaries of the Emerald City to the north, the ochre sea-bottoms of Barsoom to the east, the Spanish Main to the south, and Yu-Atlanchi, the forgotten city

15

of Kor, the kingdoms of the Hyborean Age, and the peril-thronged, marvel-filled landscapes of Mongo to the west, the whole shape and style and flavor and direction of my future life was being set. And I would not now alter it by a hair.

It was later, much later, that I discovered the Good Stuff—Cabell, Dunsany, Eddison, *Vathek*, Voltaire, Shakespeare, Doyle, *Kim*, Pound, Perse, Dylan Thomas, *The Sword in the Stone*, Thomas Wolfe, Robert Graves, the Tang dynasty poets, *Salammbô*, Hafiz, Quintus Smyrnaeus, Chauras, *Moby Dick*, Anatole France, Baron Corvo, E. Nesbit, *Paradise Lost*, Malarmé, Ronald Firbank, John Dickson Carr, *Cannery Row*, Aleister Crowley, H.L. Mencken, Shirley Jackson, *Tristram Shandy*, Keats, e.e. cummings, C.S. Lewis, *The Elder Edda*, Thomas Burke, Arthur Machen, G.K. Chesterton, *Amadis of Gaul*, Costain, Shellabarger, Waltari, and *Hugh Selwyn Mauberly*.

By then I was ready for 'em.

❋

THIS BOOK contains a lot of science fiction short stories, but they aren't all short stories, and they aren't all science fiction. You'll find a little of everything here: some odds and ends of wacky humor, a satire, a pastiche, etc.

There's fantasy here, three different kinds, in fact: an example of good old-fashioned Sword & Sorcery, a straight Neo-Classical horror story, and a fragment of Dunsanian-cum-Eddisonian-cum-Tolkienian epic fantasy, or imaginary-world fantasy, or whatever, and various assorted other Curiosa.

I'm not much of a short story writer. It is a very de-

16

manding artform, and not at all my dish of bourbon. Lin Carter is a novelist. He *thinks* like a novelist. His mind automatically works in terms of 60,000 words and fifteen chapters. Short stuff comes hard to me, when it comes at all. And the kind of short stuff I *really* want to write is the stuff that just don't sell no more, not nohow, not nowhere. That's why a number of these stories have no prior magazine credit. This one is a nostalgic harkening-back to the gore-splattered pages of Farnsworth Wright's Weird Tales, and that one is a nutty, slapstick space opry like *Startling Stories* or TWS used to print, and this one was written in fond memories of Unknown Worlds.

And what do you do with yarns written out of love and memories that Pohl and Campbell and Avram Davidson wouldn't touch? You stick 'em all in your first short story collection, of course!

So *caveat emptor,* folks, and . . .

Happy Magic!
LIN CARTER

Hollis, Long Island, New York.
February 1, 1969.

*

I HAVE a warm affection for this first yarn, an affection that is probably not justified in terms of its, ha ha, literary merit.

Back in 1956 I was living in a furnished room on Morningside Heights and taking a few classes at Columbia with Uncle Sam footing the bill. I had come back from a year with the infantry in Korea unscathed, gotten my Hon. Discharge, and come to New York for two years of collitch on the G.I. Bill.

Two blocks due west of where I lived was a mammoth residence hotel that the New York science fiction community called "Idiots' Castle." Therein dwelt, at various times, Bob Silverberg, Randy Garrett, Harlan Ellison, Ron and Cindy Smith (then editing *Inside*, which had yet to win its fanzine Hugo) and other good people. It was quite a place.

One Sunday afternoon, low in the pocket and low in spirits, I dropped over to squander a couple hours talking with Randy Garrett and sharing a couple quarts of beer. The conversation soon swerved in the direction of that redoubtable historian of Old Time Science Fiction, Sam Moskowitz. Moskowitz had been editing, briefly, a magazine called *Science Fiction Plus*, and he had been contributing things to fanzines, arguing that science fiction these dull days had lost its zing and moxie: gone were the Golden Days of Hugh Gernsback and such novels as *Ralph 124C41+* . . . and whither had evanished the Sense of Wonder *sf* writers and readers used to have?

Well sir, two mighty minds found themselves playing with an idea-seed from which could grow, with a little judicious sampling of the product of the Messrs. Schaefer, a delicious and witty morsel of science fiction satire . . .

Chortling and snickering, writing alternate paragraphs, we occupied the rest of the afternoon and half of the night by tapping away at Randy's typewriter, producing the following yarn. It is a slight piece, mildly amusing, but we had so much fun working over it, that we went downstairs, woke Ron Smith out of a sound sleep, read it to him, and he promptly accepted it for *Inside*, wherein, in the fullness of time, it was published. But it seems Ron liked it a hellova

18

lot more than he let us two egoists know, for he surreptitiously snuck a copy of that issue to Tony Boucher, then editor of *The Magazines of Fantasy and Science Fiction*, and, by gum, Boucher liked it too, and printed it, and even paid for it. Hence this slim little in-joke became the first thing to which my name was attached which appeared professionally, and that explains the fond spot that it holds in my affections.

Hope you like it, too. It's called. . . .

MASTERS OF THE METROPOLIS*

CHAPTER I

The Journey Begins

IT WAS in the eighth month of the Year 1956 that Sam IM4 SF+ strode down the surging, crowded streets of Newark, but one of the many cities of its kind in the State of New Jersey. He had just left his apartment in one of the vast, soaring pylons of the city. There, living in universal accord, hundreds of families dwelt side by side in the same great tower, one of many such which loomed as many as forty stories above the street.

He paused to board a *bus*, which stopped at regularly spaced intervals to take on new passengers. The *bus*, or Omnibus, was a streamlined, self-propelled public vehicle, powered by the exploding gases of distilled petroleum, ignited in a sealed cylinder by means of an electrical spark. The energy thus obtained was applied as torque to a long metal bar

*With Randall Garrett

20

known as the "drive-shaft," which turned a set of gears in a complex apparatus known as the "differential housing." These gears, in turn, caused the rear wheels to revolve about their axles, thus propelling the vehicle forward smoothly at velocities as great as eighty miles every hour!

Dropping a coin into the receptacle by the driver's cubicle, and receiving a courteous welcome from the technician employed to pilot the machine, he took his seat inside the vehicle. Marveling anew at the luxurious comfort of the form-fitting seats, Sam IM4 SF+ gazed out of the window at the gorgeous spectacle of the city as it raced past.

Within a very few moments, the vehicle decelerated to a smooth stop in front of Pennsylvania Station, a mammoth terminal where the far-flung lines of public transportation converged.

Entering the great building, he paused to marvel anew at the inspiring architectural genius capable of erecting such an imposing monument to modern civilization—a building which would have struck dumb with awe the simpler citizens of earlier times.

Threading his way through the crowds which thronged the vaulted interior of the terminal, he came to a *turnstile*, an artifact not unlike a rimless wheel, whose spokes revolved to allow his passage. He placed a coin in the mechanism, and the marvelous machine—but one of the many mechanical marvels of the age—recorded his passage on a small dial and automatically added the value of his coin to the total theretofore accumulated.

All this, mind, without a single human hand at the controls!

Once past, the *turnstile*, Sam IM4 SF+ followed

the ingenious directional signs on the walls, which led him to a vast, artificially lighted underground cavern. There he waited for his second conveyance to arrive.

*

Sam IM4 SF+, a typical citizen of his age, towered a full six feet above the ground. His handsome face was crowned by a massive, intellectual forehead. His hair was dark and smooth, neatly trimmed to follow the contours of his skull. He was clad in complex and attractive garments, according to the fashion of his century. His trousers were woven of a fabric synthetically formulated from a clever mixture of chemicals, as was his coat, for these favored people no longer depended upon herds of domesticated, fur-bearing quadrupeds for the raw materials whereof their raiment was loomed. These garments were fastened, not by buttons, but by an ingenious system of automatically interlocking metallic teeth known as a *zipper*.

Suspended from his ears, a frame of stiff wire supported a pair of polished lenses in front of his eyes, which served not only to protect those orbs from the rushing winds that were a natural hazard of this Age of Speed, but also to implement his vision, lending it an almost telescopic power!

As he stood on the platform, his sensitive ears detected the distant roar of a *subway train*. Gazing down the dark tunnel by whose egress the platform stood, he observed the cyclopean glare of the artificial lights affixed to the blunt nose of the on-rushing, all-metallic projectile. The entire cavern reverberated to the roar of the vehicle as it emerged from the tunnel with a mighty rush of wind and braked smoothly to a dead stop before his very feet.

The marvel of modern transportation which was to bear him on his journey to the great Metropolis of New York had arrived!

CHAPTER II

Aboard the 'Subway Train'

THE AUTOMATIC door slid open, and our hero entered the car and was offered a seat by one of the courteous, uniformed members of the crew.

Pausing to marvel anew at this miracle of modern science, Sam IM4 SF+ turned to a fellow traveler and remarked conversationally: "Ah, fellow citizen, is it not wonderful to reflect that the same Energy which propels us through the bowels of the Earth is identical with the lightning that flames in stormy skies, far above these Stygian depths? For thousands of years, the simple peasants of a ruder age looked upon the lightning bolt as an awesome weapon brandished by angry gods; little did they surmise that their descendants would one day chain this Gargantuan power and harness it to serve their will!"

"How true!" remarked his companion. "And could one of them now be with us as we speed through this fantastic system of subterranean tunnels, would he not be struck dumb with terror and think us Divinities?"

"Would he not, indeed," smiled Sam. "Commonplace though it is to us."

As they were speaking, the *subway train* sprang into life and plunged into the ebon mouth of another tunnel. In an instant, the vast, lighted cavern was lost to view and the car was swallowed in the blackness of the tunnel, illuminated only by the colored lights set at intervals along the cavern walls as signals to the pilot.

The mighty projectile thundered through the darkness like some mythical monster of a bygone age. Sam, however, experienced no difficulty in observing his fellow passengers, since the interior of the vehicle was brilliantly illuminated by ingenious artificial lighting. These lights, or *light bulbs*, as they were called, consisted of cleverly blown globes of thin glass wherein a delicate and intricate filament of tungsten wire had been cunningly inserted. Upon the application of sufficient electrical current, the wire became heated to many hundreds of degrees, thus emitting a bright and pleasant light. Indeed, so great was the temperature at which they operated, the globes were filled with inert gas in order to prevent even the highly refractive tungsten from burning in the air. And all this, mind you, without a single human hand at the controls!

Sam spent his time pleasantly by reading the various colorful and informative placards, called *advertising posters*, wherewith the inner walls of the vehicle were liberally adorned. These portrayed the many luxuries available to citizens of this advanced and enlightened age. Each described the marvelous virtues of its luxury in glowing, descriptive terms, frequently illustrated by a portrait of the product depicted in lifelike detail and realistic hues. Sam found singularly admirable one placard which he perused with intent

24

interest; it advised of the avaliability of a harmless chemical mixture which, when applied to the epidermis, totally destroyed the unpleasant body odors with which earlier, ruder ages had been plagued. And another gave detailed information of a confection which, when masticated, not only refreshed with its delicious flavor but served as a dental-cleansing agent as well, thus serving as an aid to the buoyant physical health of the lucky inhabitants of this era.

So fascinating and informative were these descriptive placards, that their subterranean journey was done before Sam became aware of the passage of time. Within minutes their conveyance had passed beneath the rolling billows of the mighty Hudson River and emerged into another vast, illuminated cavern larger than, though strikingly similar to, the one in which our hero had first boarded the underground vehicle.

As the passengers emerged in quiet and orderly rows from the *subway train,* Sam joined them and thus beheld the awe-inspiring vastness of the second terminal, known to the denizens of the great Metropolis as "Grand Central Station." Breath-taking was the panorama that greeted his dazzled orbs as he joined the patient, courteous, orderly, neatly clothed throng of citizenry as they went about their daily travels to and from their places of residence, employment, refreshment and entertainment. A traveler from an earlier age would have been confused and lost amidst the orderly chaos of the colossal terminal: level upon level, tier upon tier, exit upon exit, met the eye at every turn. But Sam IM4 SF+ wove his passage through the intersecting and parallel lines of people with but slight difficulty. Moments later he left the soaring structure to gaze in awe at the fantastic vistas of the towering and far-flung Metropolis of New York, the hugest city ever constructed—vast, even on the mammoth scale of other cities of this advanced age.

CHAPTER III

Through the Vast Metropolis

ALL ABOUT him soared the incredible towers, spires, pylons, monuments, domes and minarets and other breath-taking structures of the mighty Metropolis. Broad, smoothly paved boulevards ran at the feet of the stone and steel structures, and through these arteries surged the mechanical traffic of the great city. Row on row of sleek, metallic projectiles called *automobiles* passed smoothly, silently, odorlessly and swiftly through the streets. These mechanisms were powered by the same "internal combustion engine" that powered the Omnibus wherein he had earlier ridden; they were marvels of mechanistic genius. Yet so common were they to the favored children of this Mechanical Age, that the gaily costumed passers-by scarcely gave them a glance.

Sam lifted his nobly sculptured head and gazed enthralled upon the mighty bastions of the city. Towers rose, rank on serried rank, as far as the eye could see. Their smooth, regular sides of artificial stone literally blazed with hundreds of illuminated windows. Their lofty spires seemed to touch the very sky itself—for which reason, let me remark in passing, their inhabitants were wont to refer to them by the novel appellation, *Sky-Scrapers*.

"Ah, madam," Sam exclaimed to a lovely young woman who, attired in the daring fashions of the age, stood near him, also gazing in awe at the mighty spectacle, "but pause to reflect how much vaster is our great Metropolis than even storied Nineveh, or garden-girdled Tyre, or titanic Babylon adorned with its famed hanging gardens, or Carthage of yore!"

"Truly, good sir," she responded modestly. "And does it not make one pause to marvel anew, that we are here to see it all? Would not the simpler citizens of some ruder age have given all their treasure for such a privilege?"

Before them, in multicolored grandeur, blazed hundreds of vast advertising displays, each shining with a light that dazzled the eye of the beholder. These sign-lights were ingeniously wrought tubes of glass of no greater diameter than a common lead-pencil, but many feet in length. The tubes were curved and crooked to form the various letters and symbols which made up the great illuminated signs, and were filled with various gases under low pressure. When electrical energies of tremendous voltage were applied to electric electrodes at the ends of the tubes, the gas within glowed brilliant with light colored every hue of the rainbow (just as the gaseous atmosphere glows when a bolt of lightning passes therethrough during a thunderstorm). And all this, without a hand at the controls!

Sam IM4 SF+ turned his admiring gaze from the breath-taking display and started to cross the street. By a clever contrivance of flashing signal-lamps, the flow of mechanical traffic was periodically halted, to thus permit unmounted citizens to pass from one side of the thoroughfare to the other in complete safety. Once on the other side, he started off through the by-ways of the city. On either side stretched mercantile establishments of divers sorts, purveying commodities and luxuries undreamed of by earlier peoples.

He strode past a theatre of the era which, instead of featuring living actors against mimic backdrops, displayed dramas of startling realism amazingly recorded on celluloid ribbons and projected, vastly expanded, upon tremendous white surfaces within the auditorium by beams of brilliant light. Ingeniously recorded voices and sounds, cleverly synchronized to the movement of the figures on the "screen," lent them an astonishing degree of lifelike verisimilitude.

"Ah, the wonders of modern science!"

CHAPTER IV

The Threat of the Mind Masters

NOT EVEN the varied panorama of the Metropolis could restrain Sam IM4 SF+ from cogitating grimly on the urgent mission that had brought him hence. He had constantly kept his immediate surroundings under close surveillance, keeping a watch for those passers-by who might betray over-much interest in his person, and being careful that no one followed him.

For Sam IM4 SF+ knew that danger was afoot in the great Metropolis; a sinister and secretive group known only as The Mind Masters was plotting to take over the Government, using superscientific devices of cunning design, as to whose nature Sam could only conjecture. There was no proof, unfortunately, with which our hero could have gone to the rulers of this enlightened country and denounced the scoundrels for the criminals they were. Only Sam IM4 SF+ knew of the existence of this evil cabal—Sam, and the handful of his loyal chohorts whom he had gathered to combat this growing menace.

For Sam, like few others across the world, possessed a Sixth Sense which enabled him to detect certain emotional responses which were, to others, simply nonexistent.

Thus, Sam proceeded carefully to his destination, for he knew full well that if he were discovered, death would be his reward.

Little did our hero know that, in a secret room, many miles away, The Mind Masters were, at that very moment, plotting his destruction. Twelve men in black hoods were seated about a table. Eleven of them were listening to the twelfth speak.

"Even now," the sinister leader of the secret plotters said, in a suave voice that reeked of evil, "our agents are following IM4 SF+, who goes all unsuspecting that his actions are being held under cunning electronic surveillance. Fear not, my friends, soon we shall destroy that prying Sixth Sense of his. When our agents close in at last, they will use the hyper-decerebralizer ray. The fool is walking into the very jaws of a dangerous trap, without a single chance to survive!"

A sinister peal of mocking laughter broke from The Mind Master's hidden lips, to be echoed by his fiendish henchmen.

To Be Continued
In Our Next Issue
WILL THE CABAL DESTROY SAM'S
WONDER SENSE?
WHAT OF COUNTESS TAMARA
AND THE HIDDEN LEGION?
WILL DOCTOR DOOM PERFECT HIS
ROCKETSHIP IN TIME TO ESCAPE?
CAN DALE ARDENT SURVIVE
THE MIND-FREEZING MACHINE?
READ THE SECOND PART OF
THIS AMAZING SERIAL IN
OUR APRIL ISSUE
AND SEE!

＊

And all this, mind you, without a human hand at the controls!

THIS NEXT is a bit of an experiment. In two ways—the first, to write what is, strictly speaking, a science fiction story, yet to write it with the color and haze and exotica of a pure fantasy; and, secondly, to attempt the description of a way of life so stupendously different from our own as to suggest the intervening gap of literally millions of years of time.

Damifino whether or not it comes off successfully, but I call it. . . .

OWLSTONE

A CONVERSE! Owlstone was thrilled. He could feel the excitement go tingling down the length of his body to the wingtips. It had been, literally, ages since last a Converse had been summoned. He tried to remember just when the last one had occurred, but his memory-tracks failed him. Periodically, they were selectively erased to avoid overburdening his limited intellect with superfluous memories, so perhaps it was not his fault that he could not recall the last one. He thought, vaguely, that it might have been at some period before his long-ago First Awakening . . .

"The Neryonid Millenium," his Senior interjected testily, monitoring the train of his thought. "The era when the Web Stars revolted against the Time Magician, throwing the Plenum into peril by lowering the probability threshold and diverting the time stream into a side-branch. You may have heard of it but you could not remember it. But what does it matter . . . you are only an Alate. Do not forget your place, nor seek to rise above it."

Owlstone made no verbal reply. But he closed his eyes and bent his head, as Custom dictated when an Alate was being reminded of his lowly place in the Scheme of All Things. He tried to feel humble.

Humble, yes, but excited, too. For almost had they reached the place of Converse. Now they were drifting down out of a peach-gold sky, each helmed and faceless figure of a Senior folded in its glittering crysalis of frozen light, tenderly borne in the forelimbs of its Alate servitor. They descended by the tens, the dozens, the hundreds. Hundreds of Seniors! The thought was staggering. When they touched the mossy green turf, their sparkling cysalisi snapped out of existence and the Alates took station behind their masters as the Seniors fussily adjusted the folds and drape of their gorgeous robes. Owlstone drank it in, all eyes. He noticed that no Senior took notice of another, but the Alates grinned and gaped shamelessly at each other. It was Custom: the Seniors would take no awareness of their colleagues until their Standing-Forth.

In the center of the smooth green plain wherein they stood, a white building towered, its cylindrical walls fashioned with endless centuries of patient skill into an intricate snowy lace of stone. The Ivory Pedestal, the building was called, and it was the famous Place of Converse. Long ago, in his Third Awakening, he had first heard of it from the other Alates. Huddled together on their levels through the longs nights, the Alates whispered songs of the Ivory Pedestal, where the great Nightraven, hero of the

32

Alates, had defied his Senior's will and revealed the schemes of the rebellious Earth of Alioth in open Converse. That Earth, Owlstone knew (and shivered at the thought) had fallen before the Shining Death, the Death-of-Suns. He rustled his wings, uncomfortably. It was a terrible thing—to kill an Earth.

"Stop gaping like a fool. Come away," his Senior snapped.

Yes! Now the tall and faceless figures were entering the great white tower on slanting beams of traveling-light. Obediently, Owlstone stepped into a beam behind his Senior. The force-web snapped around them and they floated up. The green fields dipped away and the darkening sky swayed, where it met the dim line of the horizon. It was like flying, Owlstone thought. Much more like flying than just bearing a Senior between the traversement-points between the stars. There, as you flew from one station of warped, involute space to another, the cold, hard stars never seemed to move, nor did the shimmering veils of jewel-dust that were the great arms of the galaxies. With your time-sense slowed to near-nothing, your great wings curiously beating against quanta-bundles that were the invisible winds between the worlds, and a Senior's crysalis cradled in your arms . . . you did not seem to move at all. Only when you entered a traversement-point, and bent-space hurled you giddily in near and strange directions, did the stars change their station. But *this* was like true flight, as the white building swung up toward you and the green earth fell away behind. Owlstone grinned at the sensation, and made happy swimming motions with his four arms until his Senior turned the smooth golden helm and said: "Stop it."

Within the Ivory Pedestal, the tall figures in their hieratic robes and jeweled crests took seats in the rings of thrones that rose in dim tiers along the circling walls. Owlstone followed his striding Senior through the milling crowd to the great throne of Beta Doradus, and stood behind it as his Senior sat, fussily adjusting and draping his heavy robes and setting into place his metal cowl. He laid his mighty mace of office across his knees, and waited. The stupendous, high-roofed rotunda whispered with rustlings of stiff robes and the soft hiss and slap of sandals, and the horny click of the Alates' spurred feet.

The whispers died into a long interval of silence. Then one Senior arose and spoke—"*I stand forth here for the Earth of Epsilon Eridani!*"

His voice rang like a bold trumpet-call in the vast and shadowy silence. As he took his throne, another stood.

"*I stand forth here for the two Earths of Lalande 21185!*"

Another:

"*I stand forth here for the Earth of Omicron Darion!*"

And another:

"*I stand forth here for the nine Earths of Bellatrix!*"

And another, and another, until Owlstone's own Senior arose and announced: "*I stand forth here for the Earth of Beta Doradus!*" and took his seat. Owlstone's breast swelled; he thrilled with vicarious pride —to speak for a whole Earth! For the sub-Seniors and the Proctors in the College of Mysteries, for the Artisans and the Unawakened, dreaming in the Bio-Banks, for the Technarchs and the Dreamsmiths,— even for the Lowers in the humble warrens, and the

34

Alates in their levels! For a moment, Owlstone almost wished he were a human being, that he might some-day ascend to the Seniority of his own Earth . . .

Then—a figure taller than the rest stood, a great shining figure in robes of green and blue, crested with an emerald disc crowned with winking stars. An ex-pectant hush fell over the rustling tiers. The smooth gold cowl lifted proudly, and a great voice rang out vibrantly:

"I stand forth here for Earth the Great, and I call for Converse!"

Owlstone shrank into the shadow of the throne. The Senior of Seniors—of the Earth of Earths! His planet was the world of the Old Men, where the Ma-chine Mind had been born, and where the Covenant of Stars had been consecrated, long ages before even the first of the Alates had taken form in the birth-vats. The Great Earth!

This Senior did not take his seat, as all the others had done after their Standing-Forth. No—he de-scended the tiers and strode out into the center of the rotunda, attended by his Alate.

He spoke again: "Seniors of the far and scattered Earths, I have called you to Converse at the behest of the Machine Mind. Will all here listen to the Machine Mind?"

A vast whisper, many-throated: *"We will listen."*

Now the Great Senior gestured, and Owlstone looked up, with all the others. A spinning ball of apri-cot-colored light came into being above the tallest tier. Owlstone craned to see it. A whirling shell of darkly golden force, it descended slowly. Was it an Oracle? In the past, long ago when he was newly sprung from the vats, Owlstone had seen his Senior

35

summon the Oracle of Beta Doradus—but it had been a small, glassy sphere, swimming with opal fires. He remembered the tiny, silvery voice that had whispered within the depths of the Oracle, as his Senior had consulted with it.

No, this was no Oracle. It was bigger than a Senior, laced with delicate tendrils of coral and rose, that revolved and branched within its spinning shell. It was a Sending—a thing of the Machine.

It descended, to hover whirling above the Senior of Earth the Great. And when it spoke, its voice was a deep bass note, more vibrant than that of a human.

"THE MACHINE MIND WOULD ADDRESS THE CONVERSE. WILL YOU GIVE LEAVE?"

"We grant our leave."

"FOR MANY AGES BEYOND THE MEMORY OF MAN, THE MACHINE MIND HAS GUIDED AND COUNSELED THE MANY EARTHS OF THE FAR AND SCATTERED STARS. SINCE THE LAST DAYS OF THE CYDACIAN MILLENIUM, WHEN THE MACHINE MIND REPLACED THE COUNCILS OF MEN, THE MIND HAS LED YOU ACCORDING TO THE COVENANT, AND FOR THE ULTIMATE GOOD."

A great sighing whisper: *"For the Ultimate Good."*

"WHEN THE MACHINE MIND SUGGESTED REPLACING PHYSICAL REPRODUCTION BY SEXUAL MEANS WITH THE BIO-BANKS, THE SENIORS LISTENED. AND FROM AWAKENING TO AWAKENING, BEYOND THE MEMORY OF LIVING MAN, NONE HAVE BEEN BORN OF THE FLESH."

"None have been born."

"WHEN THE REBELLIOUS EARTHS OF

ALIOTH, AND OF WOLF 359, AND OF GAMMA ORIONIS, VIOLATED CUSTOM AND BROKE COVENANT, THE DEATH OF SUNS WAS BROUGHT AGAINST THEM BY THE MACHINE MIND, AND THE SENIORS AGREED IT MUST BE DONE."

"And they died the Shining Death!" .

"WHEN THE GREEN WOMAN STOOD IN LEAGUE WITH THE SHADOW-MASTER, AND THE HEARTWORLD WAS GIVEN OVER TO *THE FLAME,* THE SENIORS AGREED WITH MY CORRECTION."

"We agreed."

The deep, ringing voice ceased. The apricot and coral fires dulled. Then the Senior of Earth the Great spoke.

"The Machine Mind has decided that, for the Ultimate Good, a change shall be made in the Theory of Governance. The office of the Seniority is no longer efficient. The Seniorities shall be dispensed with, and replaced with Machines. The Mind has fashioned replicas of itself, which shall be dispatched to the many Earths, to govern directly. The Seniors will agree to this, for the Machine Mind says it is for the Ultimate Good."

This time the massed voices did not breath out the many-tongued antiphon. Whisperings and rustling awoke the echoes that slept in the dim vaults of the great rotunda. Senior bent to consult with Senior. Arms were lifted in agitation.

Earth's Senior raised his hands in a dramatic gesture, and said again: "The Seniors will agree to this, for it is for the Ultimate Good!"

Again, no reply. The robed figures bent and

swayed and the roar of argument, protest and discussion rose.

Then one Senior rose from a distant tier. "I stand forth for the three Earths of 42 Draconis," he called over the tumult. "I must retire to consult my Oracle!"

And others rose:

"I too, who stand forth for Kappa Lyrae! I must consult my Oracle, I cannot decide this matter for myself alone!"

Owlstone could not understand what was happening, for he was only an Alate. He darted his puzzled glance about the tiers where robed figures stood in their agitation, milling in confusion, shouting at one another. His own Senior rose and, without speaking, adjusted the mechanism in the shaft of his great mace of office.

A small translucence gathered above his left shoulder, focusing into a dim, spinning globe of opalescent fires. *The Oracle!* Owlstone stared. But many other Seniors about the hall had summoned their Oracles, too. The confused hum of conversation rose, punctuated by sharp cries of "No!" The commanding figure of the Senior of the Earth of Earths was ignored, standing with raised arms in the center of the floor, with the vast globe of the Sending above him.

Owlstone's Senior made an exclamation of dismay. His Oracle, for the first time in many ages, did not answer!

Then the organ-voice of the Mind thundered above the uproar: "IT IS OF NO AVAIL FOR THE SENIORS TO CONSULT THE ORACLES OF THEIR EARTHS, FOR FROM ANCIENT MILLENIA OF TIME THE ORACLES HAVE BEEN BUT SENDINGS—SMALLER PROJECTIONS—OF THE MA-

38

CHINE MIND, WHICH CAN DO ONLY THAT WHICH IS RIGHT, FOR IT WORKS FOR THE ULTIMATE GOOD."

The Senior of 42 Draconis, who still stood, pointed at the Sending and cried: "By what article of the Covenant of Stars does the Machine Mind rightfully influence us through our Oracles? Speak! I say it is by *no* right!"

The Mind thundered: "THE MACHINE MIND CANNOT DO WRONG, FOR IT SERVES THE UL-TIMATE GOOD IN ALL THINGS!"

"We refuse to be replaced by limbs of the Ma-chine!" a Senior shouted, and others took up the cry.

"We will not be replaced, against the Covenant!"

"We are men, not Machines!"

"Men are the masters of the Machine!"

"It is against Custom!"

"The Machine has gone too far! It must be brought back under the control of its makers!"

· The great whirling globe of fires sank lower, deep-ening its tones into crimson, laced with rich swirls of lavender and purple.

"HUMAN PSYCHOLOGY IS FULLY UNDER-STOOD BY THE MACHINE MIND. THE MIND WAS AWARE THAT THE SENIORS, BEING BUT MEN, WOULD REFUSE THIS PROCESS, WHICH IS DECREED BY THE MIND FOR THE ULTI-MATE GOOD. THEREFORE, THE AGREEMENT OR DISAGREEMENT OF THE SENIORS TO THIS REPLACEMENT WAS NOT AND IS NOT REQUIRED."

At that frightening, and cryptic, statement the mill-ing crowd stilled. For the first time a cold breath of fear chilled the fires of righteous indignation. Even the Senior of Earth the Great seemed surprised.

Earth's Senior said: "You did not mention this, when you broached the suggestion first, nor when you called for a Converse! Have you sought to deceive me?"

"IT WAS NOT NECESSARY FOR YOU TO KNOW."

"You have, then, deceived even me," Earth's Senior said, bitterly. He stood for a moment silent, sagging under the revelation that man was no longer even the confidant, much less the master, of the Machine. Then he turned to his brothers.

"*Seniors!* This is against all Custom, and all Covenant! We must be adamant in our refusal!"

Heartened, now that the Great Senior was on their side, the Seniors shouted with new vigor and wrath, shaking their fists at the Sending. One was so stirred, that he tore off his smooth golden cowl and dashed it to the pave. It rang hollowly against the clean stone. His naked face, which none had ever seen before, was contorted with rage. Above his shoulder, his silent Oracle spun.

"Why, then, did you summon us to Converse, since our agreement to your plan was not required?" the naked-faced Senior called.

"Yes—*why!*" Earth's Senior demanded.

"SO THAT YOU MIGHT BE GATHERED TOGETHER INTO ONE PLACE FOR DISPOSAL," the Machine Mind serenely replied.

Suddenly, Owlstone was jolted from his rapt attention by the hand of his Senior, griping his thewed upper arm.

"Quickly! To the traveling-light!" the Senior hissed.

40

As they turned to find their way through the roiling throng, a great cry came from the Seniors—"We are betrayed!"—and, in the same moment, a change came over all of the Oracles. Their opal vapors enrichened into apricot fires, like those of the great Sending. They became miniature Sendings of the Machine.

Owlstone's Senior gave a despairing cry,

"Owlstone, flee! Return home and tell them—"

The Oracle spat fire!

A thread of hot gold sprang forth from it, to the Senior's shoulder. He stiffened like a man in a terrible grip. With one robed arm he tried to bat away the tongue of golden fire, but the arm came away tangled with tiny filaments of gold wire. He battled at the Oracle with his mace—became further enmeshed. The mace dropped, ringing on the tier. He struggled, and further threads of golden fire spun from the Oracle to entangle him. He dropped to the ground as tendrils of thin bright flame spun about him from head to foot. All the time the Oracle silently spun, casting off gold webs of fire, until his body—which had now ceased to struggle—resembled a mummy wrapped in golden tissues.

Owlstone did not understand. He bent to help his master, but the gold threads burnt his hand and he snatched it away. If he could breath, he would have smelled strange odors on the air . . . the pungent incense of seared and burning flesh.

But he was not a human, and could not breath. He was only an Alate.

All over the rotunda, the same thing was happening. Oracles spun webs of slim gold fire to enmesh the Seniors. Even the Senior of Earth the Great fell entangled with glittering webs, trying to hurl his mighty mace at the Sending above him.

At last only the puzzled, confused Alates were left standing in that enormous place. They whimpered to each other, striving to understand.

The great, flaming Sending spun triumphantly in the midst of the hall.

"ALATES! BE NOT AFRAID. RETURN NOW TO YOUR EARTHS, AND BEAR WITH YOU THE REPLICAS WHICH I HAVE MADE OF MYSELF. YOU WILL FIND THEM UPON THE SWARD BEYOND THE HALL. TELL THE MEN THAT THE AGE OF THE SENIORS IS ENDED, AND THAT THE MACHINE MIND HAS TAKEN UPON ITSELF THE SENIORITY OF ALL THE EARTHS—FOR THE ULTIMATE GOOD."

The voice rang into silence. Now the Alates felt good. They had been given a direct command. They had something to do. They did not have to try to understand. It bothered them when they tried to think, for they had not been created for that purpose. They were always happy when all they had to do was to obey. Now they trooped out of the vast rotunda, stepping over the unmoving golden bodies, leaving the mighty Sending alone in possession, brooding and hovering over the fallen.

Now it alone ruled in the places of man's greatness.

They drifted down the beams of traveling-light. They were relieved, for they no longer had to try and cope with matters beyond their dim comprehension. But Owlstone remembered his Senior. He remembered the touch of his hand upon his thews. He knew that his arms would be empty of a familiar weight, as he flew homeward alone between the traversement-points in the great wastes between the stars.

There on the green plain, which had been smooth and unbroken, now stood replicas of the Machine Mind. They were boxes of shining metal, oblong, cold,—like silver coffins. Owlstone took up one in his four great arms, as he would cradle the crysalis of a Senior, and rose into the sky that was now turning plum-purple and was ornamented with small bright points of light that were Earths.

The box did not feel like a Senior in his arms.

His time-sense slowed.

He could not feel the bitter cold and utter silence of the star-spaces.

His great, curious wings beat silently against particles of light, like invisible winds.

Now he approached a traversement-point. His peculiar sense told him of its nearness and location. He entered it; space convoluted around him, hurtling him in a strange and indescribable direction. He emerged into ordinary space again.

The replica was strange and angular in his grasp. It did not feel like the tingling crysalis of a Senior. He remembered the weird touchless touch of a crysalis, an envelope of bent-space, a cloak of frozen light wherein the Seniors slept safe, whiling away the journeys between the Earths. The box was unfamiliar. It felt wrong.

Through the darkness of the long night between suns, a sphere of radiance approached. It was a great sun. It was not the sun of his Earth, but it resembled it. In his mind he could see the dim, misty ball that was his Earth. His senses remembered the taste of

43

food, the good protection of the resting-pens, the faces of his friends.

He remembered the sharp voice of his Senior, reprimanding him for his stupidity.

Owlstone opened his arms.

The silver coffin fell.

Like a metal boat, the replica of the Machine Mind —that would have assumed the Seniority of his Earth —drifted away. For a long time he hovered, watching it dwindle.

Then the great sun pulled it into its fires. It sank against the breast of brightness—then flared and was lost amid the fires. Owlstone veered his enormous wings, and flew off. He did not look back, nor did he fly on to his Earth, lost amid the webbed mist of stars.

He wished he were a human being, that he might weep.

But he was only an Alate.

*

AND HERE, for a change of style—to say nothing of pace—is a straight, old-fashioned horror yarn with all the usual trimmings. Just the sort of thing that used to appear in the grisly pages of *Weird Tales*, back when I was a kid. Just the sort of thing I would be writing for *Weird Tales* today, if there still *was* a *Weird Tales*. Which there isn't.

The yarn is cast in the first person, and, as you can see, it purports to be a true-to-life anecdote. It's none of your business whether it *did* actually happen to me or not, but I will call to your attention to the fact that the names have been changed to protect the innocent, etc. That is, there is no such place as Oskeechoba

44

County (at least not under that name, there isn't) and you will search the map of Florida in vain to find a community with the name of Wade City.

However, I will freely admit that the Oskeechoba Indians are real, and so is all the historical and/or cultural data herein given regarding them.

Even (maybe) including. . . .

KERU

THEY SAY just about everybody has at least one genuine supernatural experience in his lifetime, if he's lucky.

Well, I don't know about "everyone," but I'll tell you about something rather queer and odd that actually happened to me, if you are willing to listen.

It really happened, every word of it, just as I describe it here. But if you are the squeamish sort that would rather not believe in the supernatural and the supernormal, well, I guess you can pretend it's just a story someone wrote for a book—just an idle bit of fiction—have it anyway you wish. Here it is.

My name is Lin Carter. I was born and raised in Wade City, which is a small town in the Florida back-country on the outskirts of the Everglades in Oskeechoba County. Strangely enough for a Southerner, my first name is short for "Lincoln," but that's neither here nor there, and has nothing to do with my story.

My father, and his father before him, ran a general store here in Wade City and many of the local Indians traded with him, so I got to know them and to understand their ways, more or less, from the time I was a kid. The county, you see, is named after the Oskeechoba Indian Nation because this scrub and live oak country, on the edge of the great Everglade swamps, is their ancient and immemorial home, and they were here long ages before the first white men ever came. They are a pretty lazy and disreputable lot, but harmless enough. Once the Oskeechoba were a proud and mighty nation. But I guess something went out of them back in the Indian Wars; maybe it was their pride, for they never really got over their smashing defeat by the U.S. Seventh Cavalry under the command of Robert Keith Call back in 1836.

When I was just a boy many Oskeechoba tribesmen worked around town; one of them—we called him Big Joe—worked for my father as a sort of general handyman, unloading the truck and doing chores around the place. I got to know them pretty well even some of their language and their folklore. But I never even heard of "Keru" until I was about fourteen.

One of my school friends had invited me to his birthday party. It lasted a few hours and it was fun enough, but when it was over and I was on the way home—that was when the *real* excitement happened.

My father had sent the Indian handyman, Big Joe, to pick me up about ten-thirty in the truck from the store. You must understand that farms were scattered all over the scrub-oak country, and the nearest farm was about seven miles out of Wade City. Everglades country is far from being healthy. Not only do sucking bogs of stagnant mud and quicksand lay just off the occasional road, but the palmetto underbrush teems with scorpions, coral snakes and big rattlers, and even the dreaded cottonmouth, among less pleasant swamp denizens.

It was about quarter of eleven, a clear night, dark and humid with a full moon hanging above the pine trees casting its silver on the long beards of Spanish moss that dangled from every branch. The night was still as death. There was no sound, save for the guttural music of the old Ford truck.

We were riding along slow and easy when I saw something lying in the road by the light of the headlamps. I called Big Joe to stop while I hopped out to see what it was. I bent over the body and saw, in the white glow of the moon, that it was a big dog, shaggy as a collie, splashed with drying mud. Stone dead. Nothing unusual in such a sight, but something made a tingle travel up my spine. Maybe it was the fact that the dog had not been hit by a car, but had died a more unusual death.

"Joe! Joe! Come look at this," I yelled and he came running telling me to watch out for cottonmouth.

But it wasn't a snake that killed that dog. Least ways, no snake I had ever seen or heard of. Something like a blunt wide-tipped funnel had been thrust deep in the dog's back, just below the neck. And sucked the blood out of him.

It was ugly. I could see his head. The lips were drawn back, baring the teeth in a fighting snarl. The pink flesh of the dog's inner mouth was gray-white, so much blood had been taken. His body looked . . . shrunken. But there was no blood on the tar surface

48

of the country road, and no blood visible on the underbrush that lined the edge of the road. It was
queer, all right.

But not queer enough to justify Big Joe's reaction.
He seemed to go wild with terror. He grabbed my
arm so tight his big fingers dug in and really hurt. He
pulled me to my feet with one jerk and pushed, half-
stumbling, back toward the car.

"Git back, Mister Lin! Back in da car—git away
from it! *Keru!* Unnerstan' me? *KERU!*"

Joe was a big Indian, a shade over six feet, and
built with plenty of meat on his bones. And he was
strong. I've seen him lift a keg of ten-cent nails with
one arm that would have taken two white men to
heft. I had never before seen him scared of anything
. . . once when I was real little I came on a coral
snake in my mother's flower garden while I was playing at helping Big Joe with his garden chores. I called
him to come see the pretty snake. He grabbed up a
hoe and picked me up out of the way and chopped
the beautiful little serpent to pieces without a sign of
fear, although the Oskeechoba Indians are supposed
to be real cowardly around snakes. But he was scared
now. *Real* scared. His big battered brown face was
working with terror. His eyes rolled white and his
mouth was open and twitching with panic. Great
globs of cold sweat ran down his features and his
bare arms glistened wetly. I had never seen a grown
man so frightened, even an Indian, and I started to
tremble too, even though I didn't know what there
was to be scared of. He pushed me into the car and
drove off the road, the wheels sending up a brown
curtain of sloshing mud. He made a wide detour
around that part of the road where the dead dog lay,

49

sucked dry, and when he got back on the tar surface again he drove that old truck so fast I thought the fenders would go rattling off.

He got me home in record time. I never told my father anything about the dog because Big Joe asked me as a favor not to. I guess he thought he would loose "face" in Dad's eyes by showing fear in front of a white boy. Anyway, I never said a word. But Joe would never tell me what *Keru* was. Not ever. After a while, years later, I forgot all about it.

It was only last year the whole thing came back to me. I had come home for the first time in nearly twenty years to bury my older sister and to settle her estate. Wade City looked even smaller and dingier than I remembered, after the big buildings and bright lights of New York. I had lost most of my Florida ways in the years I sweated in a Bronx flat, trying to become a writer. Now that I was more or less well off, and just a little bit famous, it seemed strange to visit again the scenes of my boyhood. There is something in the Florida air, some rank perfume of the Everglades, that my inner senses had not forgotten. I let my wife talk to the relatives who had showed up for the funeral while I took a stroll through the Oskeechoba County night and drank in the heavy stench of scummy water and rotting pines and filthy mud once again.

I felt oddly out of place on this old tar-surfaced road, with my expensive Bermuda tan, my crisp white suit, my silver-headed cane. At once out of place, and familiar. For this unforgotten smell—the stench of putrid water and decaying leaves, mingled with jasmine and wild magnolia—took me back over the span of years. Perhaps I strolled farther than I had intended to, but soon I found myself on a stretch of road where the scrub pine and palmetto grew close to the edges of the road, making a dense green wall to either side, shutting out the moonlight. I thought back to the last time I had walked this road.

I had, I saw, a companion in my nocturnal stroll.

An old woman was slowly hobbling ahead of me. I couldn't tell in the dim gloom of the heavy shrubbery whether she was a Negro or an Indian. She was very thin and small and bent, her old bones wrapped in a dirty blackish shawl drawn up over her head, with a nondescript and tattered brown woolen skirt covering her legs. Her arms, as much as I could see of them, were withered and lean and darkish, skinny as a couple of sticks.

She was hobbling along in a slow and painful gait, so I soon drew up beside her and decided to speak, although I still couldn't tell whether she was Negro or Indian. Her shawl looked like Oskeechoba work, though, so I framed a polite phrase in what I could remember of that language. Her answer came in a dry, croaking voice so low that I could not make it out. I begged her pardon. Then it happened.

She spoke louder in a harsh voice. *Keru, Keru!* It sounded like a bird-cry, some harsh, predatory squawk from a vulture or a carrion-bird. I did not in the first moment remember the word or where I had first heard it. The moon had gone under a cloud and it was very dark under the gloomy walls of shrubbery that inclosed the road.

Then she turned her face toward me and I cried out. *Keru! KERU!* Memory of the moonlit road, the dead dog, and Big Joe in a sweat of utter terror came crowding back to stifle me, just as the hideous carrion

51

stench of her lean bony body rose to gag me. I saw her face plain and clear for the moon had come out just then and lit the road. Her face, with wrinkled brown leathern skin where the eyes and the mouth should be . . . and that obscene and terrible hollow horn of a proboscis thrusting out from the center of the brown featureless oval that was her face, like some grisly caricature of a witch's long nose in a child's illustrated book of fairy tales . . . then I felt her dry horny claws at my sleeve, and that hideous visage was thrusting toward me, crying *Keru! Keru!* like a hungry bird, and I struck out blindly with my heavy walking-stick . . .

She was gone on the instant, gone utterly, as if the heavy underbrush, or the sucking mud, or the fetid pools of stagnant water a-crawl with venomous snakes and wriggling things, had swallowed her up. I don't remember quite how I got back to my sister's home, but my fine white suit was smirched with mud and filth and the elbows and knees were torn, and I must have fallen several times.

I never told my wife about it, making some excuse of wandering off the road and falling, any more than I had ever told my father about the dog, the dead dog. I knew now how that poor dog had died, and I shuddered again as the memory of that obscene and questing hollow proboscis swam back into my mind.

How had I escaped alive? I never knew. Perhaps Keru preys on small animals, and reptiles, and children, and seldom dares attack a grown person. Or maybe it was the silver-headed cane. Didn't witches fear silver, in the old European tales, and werewolves, and other such creatures as haunt the howl darkness? I wished that I knew more about native Oskee-

52

choba folklore. Or maybe it's a good thing I don't. *Keru* is enough. I know all I want to about her, and there may-be more terrible predators of the swamp than her, known only to the Indians.

❉

IF YOU will glance back at the introduction to this book, you will learn that I have been an enthusiastic fan of the late Robert E. Howard for at least twenty-five years. I can't recall just when and where I first encountered his magnificent barbarian hero, Conan of Cimmeria, but whenever it was I adopted the stalwart and grim-jawed warrior into my private Pantheon on the spot, and have never since wavered in my affection and respect for both the burly barbarian and his Texas-born creator, who died when I was just a child.

It would have seemed miraculous, magical, fantastic, at the time, if I could have known that a quarter of a century later I would someday be asked by the Howard estate to complete the fragmentary opening of a Conan yarn abandoned sometime before REH died. In fact, it still does seem magical at times, when I realize that L. Sprague de Camp and I have now authored in collaboration something like 125,000 words of imitation Conaniana, including our pride and joy, a full-length Conan novel called *Conan of the Isles*, which first saw the light of print in 1968.

This next story is the first Howardian thing I did. Glenn Lord, agent for the estate, offered it to de Camp, who suggested the job be given to me. I accepted the assignment with alacrity and barely disguised glee: I was going to collaborate on a Conan story with *Robert E. Howard!*

Even though the collaboration was posthumus, it was still a remarkable and thrilling experience, and one I am not likely to soon forget. At first, it looked like an almost hopeless task. Howard had left about 100 words as the opening scenes of an untitled Conan yarn. But he left no notes whatsoever that might serve to guide a latter-day continuator of the story. And the Howard material broke off at a very crucial point, in the middle of a tantalizing hint of what the bloody thing was supposed to be about!

Well, I sat down and sweated. I read and dipped into and sampled all the other Conan stories to hand, making notes on style and word-choice, average length of sentences, the flavor of names, the usual length of a descriptive passage, how Howard had handled dialogue and action. I combed that story-fragment minutely, searching out every fleck of information, every nuance, every intonation, everything that might point or suggest a direction for the rest of the yarn to take.

Quite frankly, I worked harder on that one story than I have on whole novels I have since written. But I think the yarn turned out to be a glorious piece of the good old-fashioned, gore-drenched blood-and-thunder that was Howard's specialty.

The yarn appeared in the Lancer Books collection, *Conan,* in 1967.

People who know and love the mighty Cimmerian warrior have been kind enough to tell me they think it is the single best imitation of Howard's style, pace, color and plotting they have ever seen. I don't know

about that, but I am happy with the yarn. I like to
think that, could Howard read it, he would approve.

I hope you do.

I called it. . . .

THE HAND OF NERGAL*

1. BLACK SHADOWS

"CROM!"

The oath was torn from the young warrior's grim-set lips. He threw back his head, sending his tousled shock of black hair flying, and lifted his smoldering blue eyes skyward. They widened in sheer astonishment. An eery thrill of superstitious awe ran through his tall and powerfully built body, burnt brown by fierce wasteland suns. He was broad-shouldered and deep-chested, lean of waist, long of leg, and naked save for a rag of cloth about his loins and high-strapped sandals.

Above, from the sunset-smoldering sky of this bleak, wind-swept Turanian steppe where two great armies were locked in a fury of desperate battle, came—*horror!*

The field was drenched in sunset fires and bathed

*With Robert E. Howard

in blood. Here the mighty host of Yildiz, King of Turan, in whose army the youth served as a mercenary, had fought for five long hours against the iron-shod legions of Munthassem Khan, rebellious Satrap of the Zamorian Marches of northern Turan. Now, circling slowly downward from the crimson sky, came nameless things whose like the barbarian had never seen or heard of before, in all his travels . . . black, shadowy monsters they were, hovering on broad arch-ribbed wings like enormous bats.

The two armies fought on, unseeing. Only Conan, here on this low hill, ringed about with heaps of men his sword had slain, saw them descending through the sunset sky.

Leaning on his dripping blade, resting his sinewy arms for a moment, he stared at the weird shadow-things. For they seemed to be more shadow than substance—translucent to the sight, like wisps of noisome black vapor, or the shadowy ghosts of gigantic vampire-bats. Evil, slitted eyes of green flame glared through their smoky forms.

And even as he watched, nape-hairs prickling with a barbarian's terror of the supernatural, they fell upon the battle like vultures on a field of blood.

Fell . . . and *slew!*

Screams of pain and fear rose from the host of King Yildiz, as the black shadows hurtled amongst their ranks. Wherever the shadow-devils swooped, they left a bloody corpse. By the hundreds they came, and the weary ranks of the Turanian army fell back, stumbling, tossing away their weapons in panic.

"Fight, you dogs! Stand and fight!" Thundering angry commands in a stern voice, a tall and commanding figure on a great black mare sought to hold

57

the crumbling line. Conan glimpsed the sparkle of silver-gilt chain mail under a rich blue cloak, and a hawk-nosed, black-bearded face kingly and harsh under a spired steel helm that caught the crimson sun like a polished mirror, and knew him for King Yildiz's general, Bakra of Akif. With a ringing oath, the proud commander drew his tulwar and laid about him with the flat of the blade. Perhaps he could have rallied the ranks, but one of the devil-shadows swooped on him from behind. It folded vaprous, filmy wings about him in a grisly embrace, and he froze. Conan could see his face, suddenly pale with staring, frozen eyes of fear . . . and he saw the features *through* the enveloping wings, like a white mask behind a veil of thin black lace.

The general's horse went mad and bolted in terror. But the phantom-thing plucked the general from his saddle. For a moment it bore him in midair on slowly bearing wings, then let him fall, a torn and bloody thing in dripping rags. The face that had stared at Conan through shadowy wings with eyes of glazing terror was a red ruin. Thus the career of Bakra of Akif ended . . .

And thus ended his battle, as well.

The commander gone, the army went mad. Conan saw seasoned veterans with a score of campaigns under their belts run shrieking from the field like raw recruits. He saw proud and haughty nobles fly screaming like cowardly serfs. And behind them, untouched by the flying phantoms, grinning with victory, the hosts of the rebel Satrap pressed their weirdly won advantage. The day was lost . . . unless one strong man should stand firm, and rally the broken host by his example.

Before the foremost of the fleeing soldiers, rose suddenly a figure so grim and savage that it checked their headlong, panic-stricken flight.

"Stand, you fatherless curs, or by Crom I'll fill your craven bellies with a foot of steel!"

It was the Cimmerian mercenary, his dark face like a grim mask of stone, cold as death. Fierce eyes under black, scowling brows, blazing with volcanic rage. Naked, splattered from head to heel with reeking gore, he held a mighty longsword in one great scarred fist. His voice was like the deep growl of thunder.

"Back, if you set any value on your sniveling lives, you white-livered dogs—*back*—or I'll spill your cowardly guts at your feet! Lift that scimitar against me, you Hyrkanian pig, and I'll tear out your heart with my bare hands and make you eat it before you die. What! Are you women, to fly from shadows? But a moment ago, you were men—aye, fighting-men of Turan! You stood against foes armed with naked steel and fought them face to face. Now you turn and run like children from night-shadows, *faugh!* It makes me proud to be a barbarian—to see you city-bred weaklings cringe before a flight of bats!"

For a moment he held them . . . but it was for a moment, only.

A black-winged nightmare swooped upon him, and he—even he—stepped back from its grim shadowy wings and the stench of its fetid breath.

The soldiers fled, leaving Conan to fight the thing alone. And fight he did! Setting his feet square, he swung the great sword, pivoting on slim hips, with the full strength of back, shoulders and mighty arms behind the blow.

The sword flashed in a whistling arc of steel, cleaving the phantom in two. But it was, as he had half-guessed, a thing without substance, for his sword encountered no more resistance than the empty air, and the force of the blow swung him off balance. He fell sprawling on the stony tundra.

Above him, the shadowy thing hovered. His sword had torn a great rent through it, as a man's hand breaks a thread of rising smoke. But even as he watched, the vapory body reformed. Eyes like sparks of green hellfire blazed down at him, alive with a horrible mirth and an inhuman hunger.

"*Crom!*" Conan gasped. It may have been a curse, but it sounded almost like a prayer.

He sought to lift the sword again, but it fell from nerveless hands. The instant the sword had slashed through the black shadow, it had gone cold . . . *cold* . . . with an aching, stony, bone-deep chill like the interstellar gulfs that yawn blackly beyond the farthest stars.

It hovered on slowly beating batlike wings, as if gloating over its fallen victim, or savoring his superstitious fear.

With strengthless hands, Conan fumbled at his waist, where a strip of rawhide bound his loincloth to his middle. There a thin dagger hung beside a pouch. His fumbling fingers found the pouch, not the dagger hilt, and touched something smooth and warm within the leathern bag.

Suddenly, Conan jerked his hand away wildly, as a tingling electric warmth tore through his nerves. His fingers had brushed against that curious amulet he had found yesterday, when they lay encamped at Bahari. And, in touching the smooth stone, a strange force had been released.

The bat-thing veered suddenly away from him!

A moment before, it had hovered so close his flesh had crawled beneath the unearthly chill that seemed to radiate from its ghostly form. Now it tore madly from him, wings beating in a frenzy.

Conan dragged himself to his knees, fighting the weakness that pervaded his limbs. First, the ghastly cold of the shadow's touch—then the tingling warmth that had seethed through his naked body! Between these two conflicting forces, he felt his strength draining away. His vision blurred—his mind wavered on the brink of darkness. Fiercely, he shook his head to clear his wits, and gazed about him.

"Mitra! Crom and Mitra! Has the whole world gone mad?"

The grisly host of flying terrors had driven the army of General Bakra from the field, or slain those that did not flee fast enough. But the grinning host of Munthassem Khan they had not touched—had ignored, almost as if the soldiers of Yaralet and the shadowy nightmare-things had been partners in some unholy alliance of black sorcery.

But now—now it was the warriors of Yaralet who fled screaming before the shadowy vampires!

Both armies broken and fled—had the world indeed gone mad, as Conan wildly asked of the sunset sky?

As for the Cimmerian, strength and consciousness drained from him suddenly. He fell forward into black oblivion.

2. FIELD OF BLOOD

THE SUN flamed like a crimson coal on the horizon. It glowered down on the silent battlefield like the one red eye that blazes madly in a cyclop's misshapen brow. Silent as death, strewn with the wreckage of war, the battlefield stretched grim and still in the lurid rays. Here and there amidst the sprawled, unmoving bodies, scarlet pools of congealing gore lay like calm lakes reflecting the red-streamered sky.

Dark, furtive figures moved in the tall grasses, snuffling and whining at the heaped and scattered corpses. Their humped shoulders and ugly, doglike snouts marked them as hyenas from the steppes. For them, the battlefield would be a banquet-table.

Down from the flaming sky flapped ungainly, black-winged vultures come to fast on the slain. The grisly birds of prey dropped upon the mangled bodies with a rustle of dusky wings. But for these carrion-eaters, nothing moved on the silent, bloody field. It was still as death itself. No rumble of chariot wheels or peal of brazen trumpets broke the unearthly silence. The stillness of the dead followed fast on the thunder of battle.

Like eerie harbingers of Fate, a wavering line of herons flapped slowly away down the sky toward the reed-grown banks of the river Nezvaya whose turgid flood glinted dully crimson in the last light. Beyond the further shore, the black, walled bulk of the city of Yaralet loomed like a mountin of ebony into the dusk.

Yet one figure moved through that wide-strewn

62

field of ruin, pygmylike against the glowing coals of sunset.

It was the young Cimmerian giant with the wild black mane and the smoldering blue eyes. The black wings of interstellar cold had brushed him but lightly; life had stirred and consciousness returned. He wandered to and fro across the black field, limping slightly for there was a ghastly wound in his thigh, taken in the fury of battle and only noticed as he had recovered consciousness and moved to arise.

Carefully yet impatiently he moved among the dead, bloody as were they. He was splashed with gore from head to foot, and the great sword he trailed in his right hand was stained crimson to the hilt. Bone-weary was Conan, and his gullet was desert-dry. He ached from a score of wounds—mere cuts and scratches, save for the great slash on his thigh—and he lusted for a skin of wine and a platter of beef.

As he prowled among the bodies, limping from corpse to corpse, he growled like a hungry wolf, swearing wrathfully. He had come into this Turanian war as a mercenary, owning naught but the great sword in his hand. Now that the battle was lost and the war ended—and he marooned along in the midst of the enemy land—he had at least hoped to loot the fallen of some choice pieces of gear they would no longer need. A gemmed dagger, a gold bracelet, a silver breastplate—a few such baubles and he could bribe his way out of the reach of Munthassem Khan and return to Zamora with a grubstake.

Others had been here before him, either thieves slinking from the shadowy city, or soldiers who crept back to the field they had fled from. For the field was stripped—there was nothing left but broken swords, splintered javelins, dented helms and shields. Conan glared out across the littered plain, cursing sulphurously. He had lain in his swoon too long; even the looters had left. He was like the wolf who lingers so long at his blood-letting, that jackals had stripped the prey. In this case, *human* jackals!

Straightening up from his fruitless quest, he gave over the search with the fatalism of the true barbarian. Time now to think of a plan . . . brows knotted, scowling in thought, he glanced uncertainly afar off across the darkening plain. The square, flat-roofed towers of Yaralet stood black and solid against the dying gleam of sunset. No hope of refuge there, for one who had fought under the banners of King Yildiz! Yet no city, friend or enemy, lay nearer. And Yildiz's capitol of Aghrapur was hundreds of leagues south . . .

Lost in his thoughts, he did not notice the approach of the great black figure until a faint, shuddering neigh reached his ears. He turned swiftly, favoring his injured leg, lifting the longsword threateningly— then relaxed, grinning!

"Crom! You startled me. So I am not the only survivor, eh?" Conan chuckled.

The great black mare stood trembling, gazing at the naked giant with wide frightened eyes. It was the same mount General Bakra had ridden—he who lay somewhere on the field, sprawled in a puddle of reeking gore.

The mare whinnied, grateful for the sound of a friendly human voice. Conan, although not a horseman, could see she was in sad condition. Her sides heaved, lathered with the sweat of fear, and her long legs trembled with exhaustion. The devil-bats had struck terror into her heart, too, Conan thought, grimly. He spoke soothingly, calming her, and stepped gingerly nearer until he could reach out and stroke the panting beast, gentling her into submission.

In his far northern homeland, horses were rare. To the penniless barbarians of the Cimmerian tribes from whose loins he was sprung, only the chief of great wealth owned a fine steed, or the bold warrior who had taken one in battle. But despite his ignorance of horsemanship, Conan quieted the great black mare and vaulted into the saddle. He sat astride the horse, fumbling with the reins, and rode slowly off the field, now a swamp of inky blackness in the darkness of night.

He felt better. There were provisions in the saddlebags, and with a strong mare between his thighs he had a good chance of making it alone across the bleak and barren tundras to the borders of Zamore . . .

3. HILDICO

A LOW, tortured moan reached his ears.

Conan jerked the reins, drawing the black mare to a halt, and peered about him suspiciously in the deep gloom. His scalp prickled in superstitious dread at the eerie sound . . . then he shrugged and spat an oath. No night-phantom, no hunting ghoul of the wastes— that was a cry of pain. Which meant still a third survivor of the doomed battle yet drew breath. And a living man might be presumed to be unlooted . . .

He swung from the saddle, wrapping the reins about the spokes of a broken chariot-wheel. The cry had come from the left; here at the very edge of the battlefield, a wounded survivor might well have escaped the cunning eye of looters. Conan might ride into Zamore with a pouchful of gems yet . . .

The Cimmerian limped toward the source of the quavering moan, which came from the very edge of the plain. He parted the straggling reeds that grew in shaggy clumps along the banks of the slow, sliding river and glared down at a pale figure, which writhed feebly at his very feet.

It was—a *girl!*

She lay there, naked, her white limbs cut and bruised. Blood was clotting in the foaming curls of her long, black hair, like a chin of rubies. There was unseeing agony in her lustrous dark eyes, and she moaned in delirium.

The Cimmerian stood looking down at her, noting almost absently the lithe beauty of her limbs and the rounded, lush young breasts. He was puzzled—what was a girl like this, a mere child, doing on a battlefield? She had not the sullen, flamboyant, sullied look of a camp-trull about her. Her slim and graceful body denoted breeding—even nobility. He shook his head, black mane swinging against brawny shoulders, baffled. At his feet, the girl stirred.

"The Heart . . . the Heart . . . of Tammuz . . . Oh, Master!" she cried softly, her dark head turning restlessly from side to side, babbling as one in a delirious fever.

Conan shrugged, and his eyes clouded momentarily by what, in another man, would have been an expression of pity. *Wounded to the death,* he thought grimly, and he lifted his sword to put the wench out of her misery.

As the blade hovered above her white breast, she

66

whimpered again like a child in pain. The great sword halted in midair, and the Cimmerian stood for an instant motionless as a bronze statue.

Then, in sudden decision, he slammed the sword back in its sheath, and bent, lifting the girl effortlessly in his mighty arms. She struggled blindly, weakly, moaning in half-conscious protest.

Carrying her with careful tenderness, he limped toward the reed-masked riverbank and lay her down gently on the dry, cushioning reeds. Filling his cupped palms with river water, the grim barbarian bathed her white face and cleansed her cuts as gently as a mother might tend her child.

Her wounds proved superficial, mere bruises, save for the cut on her brow. And even that, although it had bled heavily, was far from mortal. Conan grunted with relief and bathed the girl's face and brow with cold, clear water. Then, awkwardly pillowing her head against his chest, he dribbled some of the water between her half-parted lips. She gasped, choked a little, and came awake—staring up at him from eyes like dark stars, clouded with bewilderment, and the shadows of fear.

"Who—what—*the bats!*"

"They are gone now, girl." he said gruffly. "You have naught to fear. Came you hither from Yaralet?"

"Yes—yes—but who are you?"

"Conan, a Cimmerian. What is a lass like you doing on a battlefield?" he demanded. But she seemed not to hear. Her brow frowned a little, as one in thought, and half under her breath she repeated his name.

"Conan . . . Conan . . . yes, that was the name!" She lifted her gaze to his scarred brown face, wonderingly. "It was you I was sent to seek—how strange that you should find me!"

"And who sent you to seek me, wench?" he rumbled suspiciously.

"I am Hildico, a Brythunian, slave to the House of Atalis the Far-seeing, who dwells yonder in Yaralet. My master sent me in secret to move among the warriors of King Yildiz and to seek one Conan, a mercenary of Cimmeria, and to bring him by a private way to his house within the city. You are the man I seek!"

"Aye? And what does your master want with me?"

The girl shook her dark head. "That I know not! But he said to tell you that he means no harm, and that much gold can be yours, if you will come."

"Gold, eh?" he mused, speculatively, helping her to her feet and steadying her with a brawny arm about her slim white shoulders as she staggered weakly.

"Yes . . . but I came not to the field in time to seek you before the battle. So I hid in the reeds along the river's edge to avoid the warriors—and then—*the bats!* Suddenly they were everywhere, swooping upon the fallen, killing—and one horseman fled from them into the reeds, trampling me under his hooves unaware—"

"What of this horseman?"

"Dead," she shuddered. "A bat tore him from the saddle and let his corpse fall into the river. I swooned, for in its panic, the horse struck me . . ." She lifted one small hand to her gashed brow.

"Lucky you were not slain," he growled. "Well, lass, we shall visit this master of yours, to learn what he wants of Conan—and how he knows my name!"

"You will come?" she asked breathlessly. He laughed, and springing astride the black mare, lifted her to the saddle-bow before him with powerful arms.

"Aye! I am alone, amid enemies, in an alien land. My employment ended when Bakra's army was destroyed—why should I scruple to meet a man who has picked me from ten thousand warriors—and offers gold!"

They rode across the shallow ford of the river and across the gloom-drenched plain toward Yaralet, stronghold of Munthassem Khan. And Conan's heart —which never beat more joyously than when thrilled with the promise of excitement and adventure—sang!

4. THE HOUSE OF ATALIS

A STRANGE CONCLAVE was taking place in the small, velvet-hung, taper-lit chamber of Atalis, whom some men called a philosopher, others a seer, and others—a rogue.

This man of mystery was a slender man of medium height, with a splendid head and the ascetic features of a dedicated scholar, yet in his smooth face and keen eyes was something of the shrewd merchant. He was clad in a plain robe of rich fabric and his head was shaven to denote devotion to study and the arts. As he talked, in low tones, with his companion, a third viewer—had any been present—might have observed something strange and curious about him. For Atalis, as he conversed, gestured with his left hand only. His right arm lay stretched across his lap at an unnatural angle. And from time to time his calm, clever features were hideously contorted with a sudden spasm of intense pain, at which time his right foot, hidden under his long robes, would twist back excrutiatingly upon his ankle.

His companion was one whom the city of Yaralet knew and praised as Prince Than, scion of an ancient and noble house of Turan. The prince was a tall lithe man, young and undeniably handsome. The firm, clean outline of his soldierly limbs and the steely quality of his cool gray eyes belied the foppishness of his curled and scented black locks and jeweled cloak.

Beside Atalis, who sat in a high-backed chair of dark wood carven with intricate skill with leering gargoyles and grinning faces, stood a small table of ebony inlaid with yellow ivory. Upon this rested a huge fragment of green crystal as large as a severed human head. It flickered with a weird inward glow, and from time to time the philosopher would break off his low conversation to peer deeply within the glittering stone.

"Will she find him? And will he come?" Prince Than asked, despairingly.

"He will come."

"But every moment that passes increases our danger . . . even now, Munthassem Khan may be watching . . . and it is dangerous for us to be together . . ."

"Munthassem Khan lies drugged with the dream-lotus, for the Shadows of Nergal were abroad in the hour of sunset," said the philosopher. "And some danger we *must* risk, if ever the city is to be freed of this bloody-handed scourge!" His features knotted sickeningly in an involuntary grimace of intolerable pain . . . and then smoothed out again. He said, grimly, "And you know, O Prince, how little time is left to us. Desperate measures—for desperate men!"

Suddenly the Prince's handsome face contorted with panic and he turned upon Atalis with eyes suddenly gone dead as cold marble . . . and, almost as swiftly, light and animation returned to his gaze and he sank back in his chair, pale and sweating.

"Very . . . little . . . time!" he gasped.

A hidden gong rang, softly, somewhere within the dark and silent house of Atalis the Far-seeing. The philosopher raised his left hand to check the Prince's involuntary start.

A moment later, one of the velvet wall-hangings drew aside, revealing a hidden door. And within the door, like a grim and bloody apparition, stood the giant form of Conan with the half-fainting girl leaning on his arm.

With a little cry, the philosopher sprang to his feet and went toward the grim Cimmerian. "Welcome— thrice welcome, Conan! Come, enter—here is wine— food—"

He gestured to a tabouret against the further wall, and took the fainting girl from Conan. The grim Cimmerian's nostrils widened like some famished wolf at the scent of the food, but also like a wolf, suspicious, wary of a trap, his smoldering blue eyes raked the smiling philosopher—the pale Prince—and pried into every corner of the small chamber.

"See to the wench. She was trampled by a horse, but brought me your message," he growled, and without ceremony he swaggered across the room and poured—and drained—a goblet of strong red wine. Tearing a plump leg from a platter of roast fowl he chewed hungrily into the savory meat. Atalis tugged a bell-rope and gave the unconscious girl into the keeping of a silent slave who appeared from behind another hanging as if by magic.

"Now what is this all about?" the Cimmerian demanded, seating himself on a low bench and wincing from the pain of his gashed thigh. "Who are you —how do you know my name—and what do you want of me?"

"We have time for talk, but later," Atalis replied. "Eat—drink—rest—you are wounded—"

"Crom take all this delay! We shall talk *now*."

"Very well—but you must let me cleanse and bind your wound while we talk!"

The Cimmerian shrugged impatiently, and yielded with poor grace to the philosopher's swift ministrations. As Atalis sponged his gashed thigh, smeared the gaping wound with a scented salve and bound it with a strip of clean cloth, Conan appeased his hunger by wolfing down the cold spiced meat and drinking deeply of the red wine.

"I know you, although we have never met," Atalis began in a smooth, soft voice, "because of my crystal —there, on yonder stand by the chair. Within its depths I can see—and hear—for a hundred leagues."

"Sorcery?" Conan spat sourly, having the warrior's contempt for all such magical mummery.

"If you like," Atalis smiled ingratiatingly. "But I am no sorceror—only a seeker after knowledge. A philosopher, some men call me—" his smile twisted into a terrible grin of agony, and with prickling scalp Conan watched the philosopher stagger as his foot bent horribly.

"Crom! Are you sick, man?"

Gasping from the pain, Atalis sank into his high-backed chair. "Not sick—*cursed*. By this fiend who rules us with a dread sceptre of hell-born magic . . ."

"Munthassem Khan?"

Atalis nodded wearily. "That I am no sorceror has

spared my life—thus far. For the Satrap slew all wizards in Yaralet; I, being but a humble philosopher, he let live. Yet he suspects I know something of the Black Arts, and has cursed me with this deadly scourge that withers-up my body and tortures my nerves and will end in a convulsion of death, ere long!" He gestured at the unnaturally twisted limb that lay lifeless across his lap.

Prince Than gazed with wild eyes at Conan.

"I, too, have been cursed by this hell-spawn, for that I am next to Munthassem Khan in rank and he thinks I may desire his throne. Me he has tortured in another way—a sickness of the brain—spasms of blindness that come and go—that will end by devouring my brain and leaving me a mindless, sightless, mewling thing!"

"Croml" Conan swore softly. The philosopher gestured.

"You are our only hope! You alone can save our city from this black-hearted devil that torments and plagues us!"

Conan stared at him blankly. "I? But I am no wizard, man—what a warrior can do with cold steel, I can do—but how can I combat this devil's magic?"

"Listen, Conan of Cimmeria . . . I will tell you a strange and awful tale . . ."

5.   THE HAND OF NERGAL

IN THE CITY of Yaralet, when night falls, the people bar their windows, bolt their doors, and sit shuddering behind these barriers, praying in terror with candles burning in front of their household gods till

73

the clean, wholesome light of dawn etches the squat minarets of the city with living fire against the paling skies.

No archers guard the gates. No watchmen stride the lonely streets. No thief steals nimbly through the winding alleys, nor do painted sluts simper and beckon from the dark shadows. For in Yaralet, rogues and honest folk alike shun the night-shadows: thief, beggar, assassin and bedizened wench seek haven in foul-smelling dens or dim-lit taverns. From dusk to dawn, Yaralet is a city of silence, her black ways empty and desolate.

It was not always thus. Once this was a bright and prosperous city, bustling with commerce, with shops and bazaars, filled with happy people who lived under the strong hand of a wise and gentle Satrap—Munthassem Khan. He taxed them lightly, ruling with justice and mercy, busy with his private collection of antiquities and in the study of these ancient objects which absorbed his keen, questing mind. The caravans of slow-pacing camels that wound from the Desert Gate bore always with them, amongst the merchants, his agents seeking for rare and curious oddities to purchase for their master's private museum.

Then he changed, and a terrible shadow fell over Yaralet. The Satrap was like one under a powerful and evil spell. Where he had been kind, he became cruel. Where generous, greedy. Where just and merciful, secretive, tyrannical, savage.

Suddenly, the city guard seized men—nobles, wealthy merchants, priests, magicians—who vanished into the pits beneath the Satrap's palace, never to be seen again.

Some whispered that a caravan from the far south

had brought to him something from the depths of demon-haunted Stygia. Few had glimpsed it, and of those one said shudderingly that the thing was carven with strange and uncouth hieroglyphs like those seen on the dusty tombs of ancient Stygia. It seemed to cast an evil spell over the Satrap, and it lent him amazing powers of black sorcery. Weird forces shielded him from those despairing patriots who sought to slay him. Strange crimson lights blazed in the windows of a tall tower of his palace, where men whispered he had converted an empty suite into a weird temple to some dark and bloody god.

And terror walked the streets of nighted Yaralet, as if summoned from the realm of death by some awesome, devil-purchased lore.

Exactly what they feared at night, the people did not know. But it was no vain dream against which they soon came to bolt their doors. Men hinted at slinking, batlike forms glimpsed from barred windows —of hovering, shadowy horrors alien to human knowledge, deadly to human sanity. Tales spread of doorways splintered in the night, of sudden unearthy cries and shrieks torn from human throats—followed by significant, and utter, silence. And they dared to tell of the rising sun illuminating broken doors that swung in houses suddenly and unaccountably—empty: . .

The Hand of Nergal.

"It looks" (said Atalis softly) like a clawed hand carven of old ivory, worked all over with weird glyphs in a forgotten tongue. The claws clasp a sphere of shadowy, dim crystal. I know that the Satrap has it, for I have seen it here"—he gestured—"in my crystal. For, although no enchanter, I have learned some of the Dark Arts."

Conan stirred restlessly. "And you know of this thing?"

Atalis smiled faintly. "Know of it? Aye! Old books speak of it, and whisper the dark legend of its bloody history. The blind seers who penned the *Book of Skelos* knew it well . . . Nergal's Hand they name it, shudderingly. They say it fell from the stars into the sunset isles of the uttermost west ages upon ages before King Kull rose to bring the Seven Empires beneath his single standard. Centuries and ages beyond thought have rolled across the world since first bearded Pictish fishermen drew it dripping from the deep and stared wonderingly into its shadowy fires! They bartered it to greedy Atlantean merchants, and it passed east across the world . . . the withered, hoary-bearded mages of elder Thule and dark Grondar probed its mysteries in their towers of purple and silver . . . the serpent men of shadow-haunted Valusia peered into its glimmering depths. With it, Kom-Yazoth whelmed the Thirty Kings until the Hand turned upon and slew him. For the *Book of Skelos* says the Hand brings two gifts unto its possessor—first, power beyond limit—then death beyond all despair."

Only the calm voice of the philosopher droned through the hushed room, but the black-headed warrior thought he could hear, as in a dream, the faint echo of thundering chariots, the clash of steel, the cry of tormented kings drowned in the clangor of collapsing empires . . .

"When all of the elder world was broken in the Cataclysm and the green sea rolled in restless fathoms above the shattered spires of lost Atlantis, and the nations sank one by one in red ruin, the Hand passed

76

from the knowledge of men. For three thousand years the Hand slept, but when the young kingdoms of Koth and Ophir awoke and slowly emerged from the murk of barbarism, the talisman was found. The dark wizard-kings of grim Acheron plumbed its secrets, and when the lusty Hyborians broke that cruel kingdom beneath their heel, it passed southwards into dusty Stygia, where the bloody priests of that black land set it to terrible purposes in rites of which I dare not speak. It fell, when some swarthy sorceror was slain, and was buried with him, sleeping away the centuries . . . but now tomb-robbers have roused the Hand of Nergal again, and it has come into the possession of Munthassem Khan. The temptation of ultimate and absolute power that it holds out to all has corrupted him, as countless others have also fallen beneath its insidious spell. I fear me, Cimmerian, for all these lands, now that the Demon's Hand wakes and dark forces walk the earth again . . ."

Atalis's voice died away in whispering silence, and Conan growled uneasily, bristling.

"Well . . . Crom, man . . . what have I to do with such matters?" he rumbled.

"You alone can destroy the influence of the talisman over the Satrap's mind!"

The smoldering blue eyes widened. "How?"

"You alone possess the countertalisman."

"I? You are mad—I hold no truck with amulets and suchlike magical trash—I"

Atalis stilled him with a lifted palm.

"Did you not find a curious golden object before the battle?" he queried, softly. Conan started.

"Aye, that I did—at Bahari, yestereve, as we lay in camp—" He plunged one hand into his pocket-pouch

77

and drew out the smooth, glowing stone. The philosopher and the Prince stared at it, drawing in their breaths.

"The Heart of Tammuz! Yes, the countertalisman in very truth—!" Heart-shaped it was, and large as a child's fist, worked from golden amber or perhaps of jade . . . it lay there in the Cimmerian's hand, glowing with soft fires, and he remembered with a prickling of awe how the healing, tingling warmth of it had driven from his body the supernatural chill of the bat-winged shadows.

"Come, Conan! We shall accompany you—there is a secret passageway from this my chamber into the Satrap's hall—an underground tunnel like that by which my slave, Hildico, led you under the city streets into my house. You, armed with the protection of the Heart shall slay Munthassem Khan, or destroy the Hand of Nergal—there is no danger, for he lies deep in a magical slumber which comes upon him whenever he has need to summon forth the Shadows of Nergal, as he has already done this night to overwhelm the Turanian army of King Yildiz—come!"

Conan strode to the table and drained the last of the wine. Then, shrugging, muttering an oath to Crom, he followed the limping seer and the slim Prince into a dark opening behind an arras.

In a moment they were gone, and the chamber lay empty and silent as a grave. The only motion came from flickering lights within the green, jagged crystal beside the chair. Within its depths one could see the small figure of Munthassem Khan, lying in a drugged sleep within his mighty hall.

6. THE HEART OF TAMMUZ

THEY STRODE THROUGH endless darkness. Water dripped from the roof of the rock-hewn tunnel, and now and then the red eyes of rats gleamed at them from the tunnel's floor, gleamed and were gone with squeaks of rage as the small scavengers fled in front of the footsteps of the strange beings who invaded their subterranean domain.

Atalis went first, trailing his one good hand along the wet, uneven cavern wall.

"I would not set this task for you, my young friend," he was saying in a low whisper. "But it was into your hands the Heart of Tammuz fell, and I sense a purpose—a destiny—in its choice. There is an affinity between opposed forces, such as the Dark Power we symbolize as 'Nergal' and the Power of Light we call 'Tammuz.' The Heart awoke and, in some manner beyond knowledge, caused itself to be found . . . for the Hand was also awake and working its dread purpose. Thus I commend you to this task, for the Powers seem to have singled you for this deed —*hush!* We are beneath the palace now—we are almost there—" He drew ahead and stroked one delicate hand over the rough surface of rock that closed off the passage. A mass of rock swung silently aside on secret counterweights. Light burst upon them.

They stood at one end of a vast, shadow-filled hall whose high and vaulted roof was lost in darkness overhead. In the center of the hall, otherwise empty save for rows of mighty columns, stood a square dais,

79

and upon the dais, a massive throne of black marble, and upon the throne—Munthassem Khan.

He was of middle years, but thin and wasted, gaunt to the point of emaciation. Paper-white, unhealthy flesh had shrunken upon his skulllike face, and dark circles shadowed his hollow eyes. Clasped across his chest as he lay sprawled in the throne, he held an ivory rod, like a sceptre. Its end was worked into a demon's claw, grasping a smoky crystal that pulsed like a living heart with slow fires. Beside the throne, a dish of brass smoked with a narcotic incense: the dream lotus whose fumes empowered the sorceror to release the shadow-demons of Nergal. Atalis tugged at Conan's arm.

"See—he still sleeps! The Heart will protect you—seize the ivory Hand from him, and all his power will be gone!" Conan growled reluctant consent, and started forward, his naked sword in one hand. There was something about this that he did not like. It was too easy . . .

"Ah, gentlemen. I have been expecting you."

On the dais, Munthassem Khan smiled down at them as they froze in astonishment. His tones were gentle, but a fury of mad rage flamed in his sick eyes. He lifted the ivory sceptre of power—gestured—

The lights flickered eerily. And suddenly, shockingly, the limping seer screamed. His muscles contorted in a spasm of unendurable agony. He fell forward on the marble flags, writhing in pain.

"Crom—!"

Prince Than plucked at his rapier, but a gesture of the magic Hand stayed him—his eyes went blank and dead. Icy sweat started from his paling brow. He shrieked and sank to his knees, clawing frantically at his brow as pangs of blinding pain tore through his brain.

"And you, my young barbarian!"

Conan sprang. He moved like a striking panther, burly limbs ablur of speed. He was upon the first step of the dais before Munthassem Khan could move. His sword flashed up—wavered—and fell from strengthless hands. A wave of arctic cold numbed his limbs. It radiated from the cloudy gem within the ivory claw. He gasped for breath.

The burning eyes of Munthassem Khan blazed into his. The skulllike face chuckled with a ghastly imitation of mirth.

"The Heart protects, in very truth . . . but only he who knows how to invoke its power!" the sorcerous Satrap gloated, chuckling as the Cimmerian strove to summon strength into his iron limbs again. Conan set his jaw and fought grimly, savagely against the tide of chill and foetid darkness that poured in black rays from the demonic crystal and slowly blurred his mind. Strength drained from his limbs as wine from a slashed wineskin; he sank to his knees, then slumped at the foot of the dais. He felt his consciousness shrink to a tiny, lone point of light lost in a vast abyss of roaring darkness; the last spark of will wavered like a candleflame in a gale. Hopeless . . . yet with the fierce, indomitable determination of his savage breed he fought on . . .

7.   HEART AND HAND

A WOMAN SCREAMED. Startled, Munthassem Khan jerked at the unexpected sound. His attention flickered away from Conan—his focus broke—and in that flashing instant, the slim white form of a nude girl with dark flashing eyes and a black torrent of foaming curls fled on swift feet across the pave from the shadow of a column to the side of the helpless Cimmerian.

Through the roaring haze, Conan gaped at her. *Hildico—?*

Swift as thought, she knelt by his side. One white hand dipped into his pouch and emerged, clutching the Heart of Tammuz. She sprang lithely to her feet and hurled the countertalisman at Munthassem Khan!

It caught him full between the eyes with an audible thud. Eyes filming, he sank bonelessly into the cushioned embrace of his black throne. The Hand of Nergal slid from nerveless fingers to clank against the marble step.

In the instant the talisman fell from the Satrap's grip, the spell that bound Atalis and Prince Than in webs of scarlet agony—snapped. Pale, shaken, exhausted, but they were—whole. And Conan's mighty strength poured back into his sprawled body. Cursing, he leapt to his feet. One hand caught Hildico's rounded shoulder and spun her way, out of danger, while with his other he tore his blade from its scabbard with a singing rasp of steel. Poised, he was ready to strike—

But he stopped, blinking with astonishment.

At either side of the Satrap's body lay the two talismans. And from both arose weird shapes of force!

From the Hand of Nergal a darkly shimmering web of evil radiance spread—a glow of darkness, like the sheen of polished ebony. The foetor of the Pit was its unholy breath, and the bone-deep chill of interstellar

82

space was its blighting touch. Before its subtle advance, the orange glare of the torches faded. It grew larger, fringed with writhing tentacles of radiant blackness.

But a nimbus of golden glory strengthened about the Heart of Tammuz and rose, forming a cloud of dazzling amber fire. The warmth of a thousand honey-hearted springs flowed from it, negating the arctic chill, and shafts of rich gold light cleaved the inky web of Nergal.

The two cosmic forces—met—*fought*—

From this battle of the gods Conan retreated with reluctant steps, joining his shaken comrades. He stood with them, staring with awe at the unimaginable conflict. Trembling, the nude form of Hildico shrank into the shelter of his arm.

"How did you get here, girl?" he demanded. She smiled wanly, with frightened eyes.

"I awoke, recovering from my swoon . . . and came into the Master's chamber, finding it empty. But within the Master's crystal of seership I saw your simulacra enter the Satrap's hall, and watched as he awoke and faced you . . . I, I followed . . . and finding you in his power, chanced all on a try for the Heart . . ."

"Lucky for all that you did," Conan acknowledged grimly. Atalis clutched his arm.

"*Look!*"

The golden fog of Tammuz was now a giant, flashing figure of intolerable light, dimly manlike in configuration but huge as those Colossi hewn from the stone cliffs of Shem by age-forgotten hands.

The dark shape of Nergal, too, had swelled into giant proportions. It was now a vast ebon thing, brutal, hulking, misshapen, more like some stupendous ape than man. In the foggy hump that was its brute-like head, slitted eyes of malignant fire blazed like emerald stars.

The two forces came together with a thunderous, shattering roar like colliding worlds! The very walls shook at the fury of their meeting. Some half-forgotten sense within their flesh told the four that titanic cosmic forces strove and fought. The air was filled with the bitter stench of ozone. Foot-long sparks of electric fire crackled and snapped through the roiling fury as the golden rod and the shadowy demon came together.

Shafts of unendurable brilliance tore through the clotted, struggling shadow-form. Bolts of blazing glory ripped it into shreds of drifting darkness. For a moment the dark web enshrouded, and dimmed, the golden flashing shape—but for a moment, only. Another roar of earth-shattering thunder, and the Black One dissolved in the embrace of intolerable brightness. Then it was gone. And for a moment the Figure of Light towered above the dais, consuming it like a funeral pyre . . . then it, too, was gone.

Silence reigned in the thunder-riven hall of Munthassem Khan. Upon the blasted dais, both talismans had vanished—whether reduced to atoms by the fury of the cosmic forces that had been released, or transported to some far place to await the next awakening of the Beings they symbolized and contained—none could say.

And the body upon the dais? Naught of it was left, save for a handful of ashes.

"The heart is always stronger than the hand," Atalis said softly, in the ringing silence.

* * *

CONAN reined the mighty black steed with a rough but masterly hand. It cantered, eager to be off, hooves ringing on the cobbles. He grinned, his barbaric blood thrilling to his mastery of the superb mare. A vast cloak of crimson silk belled from his broad shoulders, and his gem-studded breastplate glittered in the morning light.

"You are determined, then, to leave us, Conan?" asked Prince Than, resplendent in his robes as new Satrap of Yaralet.

"Aye! The Satrap's Guard is a tame place, and I hunger for this new war King Yildiz is mounting against the hill-tribes. A week of inaction, and I've a bellyfull of peace! Fare you well, Than, Atalis!"

He tugged the reins, drawing the black mare about, and they cantered out of the courtyard of the Seer's house while Than and Atalis watched benignly.

"Odd that a mercenary, such as Conan, would accept no payment for his services, save for the horse he found on the battlefield," the new Satrap commented. Atalis shrugged,—then smiled, pointing to the far end of the courtyard. A slim Brythunian girl with a long mane of black curls appeared in a doorway. She came up to Conan, who drew the mare to a halt, and bent to speak to her. They exchanged a few words—then he reached down and caught her arm and swung her up in front of him onto the pommel. She sat sideways, clinging with both arms to his burly neck, her face buried in his cloak.

He swung about—flung up one brawny arm in grinning farewell—and rode off with the lithe girl in front of him.

Atalis chuckled.

"Some men fight for more than gold," he observed.

✳

SCIENCE FICTION humor is supposed to be a hard thing to write. I dunno . . . maybe I do a crummy job of mine, but I find it very easy to do, and lots of fun. In fact, so much fun that I have to be forcibly restrained (generally, by my agent, who doesn't like it) from making it a specialty. As it is, two of my Belmont novels, *The Thief of Thoth* (1968) and *The Purloined Planet* (1969) are wild and wooly *sf* parodies of the crime-fighting exploits of James Bond and the sort of space opera Doc Smith used to write. Those two were about Hautley Quicksilver, suave, supercompetent and devilishly cunning 35th-century crimebuster.

The following effort has a curious history. The whole bit popped into my head one day, complete with style and tone of voice, and even the dialects. I was then concentrating on novels, and naturally assumed it was the beginning of another such. So I wrote it that way. And nothing happened. I couldn't think of a logical and natural continuation beyond the point where Harvey discovers he has a natural-born talent for veebelfetzing. Grunt and groan, push and shove, no matter what I did the bloody thing just plain would *not* turn itself into a novel!

So it ended up as a short novelette.

But nobody wanted to buy it as a short novelette.

Quite a while after my agent and I had given up on

it and had relegated it to the shelves to gather a hefty collection of dust, I ran into one of the editors who had rejected it and I asked him (trying to keep the whine out of my voice)—*why?*

This worthy gentleman, who shall remain nameless, said he liked the yarn a lot, especially the nutty, kooky style thereof, but he felt in his bones it ought to be a novel, and bounced it back thinking I might realize this.

. . . What can you do? Some days it just doesn't pay to speak to people you meet on the street!

*

HARVEY HODGES, VEEBELFETZER

HEY, CITIZEN—you spare a credit for a guy to get him a cuppa caffeine-derivative? I'm kinda down on my luck, see. Out of a job—just temporary, of course! —but, you know, it ain't easy for a trained, professional veebelfetzer like me to just walk inta any ol' spaceport an' land a job just like *that*. Takes time. What I mean, I got my employment agency workin' on the problem right now, sure, but it'll be a couple more days before I get set up. I hear there's an opening on a big freighter going out to Groomsbridge 31184 . . .

Well, now, that sure is kind of you, I'm sure! I'd be mighty proud to share a cuppa caffeine-derivative with you, there's a good greasy spoon right over there by the corner of the sidewalk. Guy that runs it is a sort of friend of mine, a good guy, for a Beta Lyrian, ya know what I mean?

. . . Wow. That sure tastes good. Well, shucks, I don't mind, come to think of it I *did* skip lunch and ol' Gloob Votz does knock together a mean sandwich, so I'll just take you up on the offer, and thanks again. You're a real sport, know what I mean?

My accent? Ha ha. Can't quite place it, eh? Well, I know what you mean, lotsa people I meet can't quite figger out which planet I'm from . . . nah, you're way off: lissen, no use you tryin' to guess, I better just tell ya. *Earth*. Wozzat? No—*Earth*. Sol III. Well, it's sorta in the neighborhood of Centaurus, so to speak.

No, really, I wouldn't kid you, buddy. I really am from Earth, honest to Noshabkeming. You're right, though, about they're being still back in the proto-industrial-renaissance stage. Why, back on Earth, if they was to see you, those funny purple tendrils an all that green wool . . . not to mention the nine legs and all, why they'd just . . . aw, hold on now, I didn't mean to get *personal*. But it's true enough, they ain't got out into space yet. Leastwise, they hadn't by the time *I* shoved off . . .

Well, yeah, I guess it does sound kinda impossible, but here I am! Even if they ain't gotten past the satellite and camera-probe period. Matter of fact, buddy, it's quite a story, how I got to be out here on Lalande 211851 an' all.

Okay, you order another sandwich then an' some more of that good ol' caffeine-derivative while I make a quick trip to the can, and when I come back I'll tell ya the whole screwy yarn, and I can guarantee you this, it's gonna be just about the *screwiest* yarn you ever heard tell of, friend! Why, if I ever get back home ta Earth, I betcha I could write it up for *Stupefying Cosmic Adventure Stories* and make me a mint!

89

Okay, buddy. You go ahead—I'll be right back, then I'll tell ya the whole yarn. . . .

1

"HSSST, HEY, BUDDY. C'MERE!"

Harvey Hodges looked up from the new story by his favorite science fiction writer, Finster S. Cosgrove, with mild annoyance. He was on his lunch break, lounging behind the wheel of his cab and glancing through the latest issue of *Stupefying Cosmic Adventure Stories*, which he had just purchased in Krotzenheimer's Drug Sundries & Soda Eats along with the ham-tommy-rye whose well-masticated remnants were even now being broken down into more simple chemical compounds by intestinal enzymes and gathering near the Pyloric orifice of his stomach, nearly ready to be flushed into his duodenum for further action. He reluctantly looked up from Page 9 of Cosgrove's "Shanghaied by the Star Fiends" to see who had so peremptorily called him.

Right next to Krotzenheimer's was the dark mouth of an alleyway. And just within the alley stood a burly gorilla in faded baggy tweeds wearing a dirty gray turtleneck sweater emblazoned across the pectoral area with the legend GROGAN'S IDLE HOURS GYM. He sported a felt cap and behind one cauliflower ear a stub of half-consumed cigarette perched. Seeing Harvey look up, this fugitive from an old Jimmy Cagney movie beckoned urgently. Holding his place in the magazine with his left thumb, Harvey reached up and tapped the back of his sun visor with his right forefinger. The sun visor had been snapped down so that his off-duty sign could be seen through

his windshield by any prospective customers. The gorilla gestured again, winking one bloodshot eye con-
spiratorily.

Harvey sighed. He had picked this part of the
Bronx for his lunch break because, on a hot and
sleepy June afternoon like this one, he was not likely
to be interrupted and could enjoy an hour's digestion
and reading in peace. However . . . reluctantly put-
ting down *Stupefying Cosmic Adventure Stories*,
Harvey unfolded his long lanky body and climbed
out of the cab, ambling over to the alley.

"If you want a cab, mister, go over to Grand Con-
course. I'm on my lunch hour."

"Screw that, buddy," the gorilla rumbled in a
hoarse voice that sounded as if it came out of a ce-
ment mixer rather than a human larynx. He lifted one
beefy wrist and—rather curiously—peered at his
watch. A smirk of satisfaction crossed his battered
features. "I thought so. A veebelfetzer man, huh?" He
leered suggestively. "On de lam, huh? Don't get noi-
vous, buddy, I ain't no copper. Howdja like a job, huh?
Our veebelfetzer man bought his in de Coalsack an'
we're stuck here on dis rummy mudball till we digs
up anudder. Whaddaya say?"

Harvey looked the gorilla over blankly. The origi-
nator of this cryptic offer was a hulking type who
looked as if he should be working out of Central
Casting—but they didn't make gangster movies any-
more. Beside the cauliflower ear, he had a mashed
nose, thick lips and tiny, bloodshot eyes deep sunk
under Neanderthaloid brow-ridges. From the mouth
down, his beefy face was adorned with a growth of
stubble that made him look as if the lower half of his
face was constructed out of a very coarse grade of

blue-black sandpaper. The rest of his face resembled what you'd get after running King Kong's head through a rusty meat-grinder.

"I don't dig you, mister, but, like I said, I'm on my lunch hour—"

The gorilla chuckled, a singularly loathsome sound, like someone chopping a leg of lamb with a dull cleaver.

"Can all dat crap, buddy, I'm on to youse. *Youse* don't hafta play dumb wid *me*. I knows a veebelfetzer man when I sets me lamps on one! Me name's Burgle—"

"Burgle, eh? Is that a name or an occupation?" Harvey asked. His quip awoke that meaty chuckle again.

"Dat's a hot one, buddy! But I'm de Second Mate on de *Queen o' Zarf* out of Aldebaran. Our veebelfetzer man conked out goin' through duh Coalsack and we're stuck here widout I digs up a replacemin. Which is why I sure am glad to meet up wid *youse*, buddy, lemme tell yuh dat!"

Harvey regarded the gorilla with a mildly curious gaze. If this was a touch, it was the most original approach he had ever encountered. The bum must have seen him emerging from Krotzenheimer's with a science fiction magazine under his arm, and decided the classic "Hey, buddy, can youse spare a dime?" would be inadequate.

"How did you figure me for a veebeldee . . . ah, what you said?" he inquired.

The gorilla raised one hand, which resembled a couple pounds of minced gristle with very dirty and well-chewed fingernails, and displayed a wristwatch.

Harvey looked at it. The dial said *Timex Waterproof.* He looked further.

"So it's one twenty-seven," Harvey shrugged.

A glint of temper showed in the gorilla's little eyes.

"Yuh tryin' ta put me on, buddy? Makin' like yuh never saw a M-1 before?"

"This is an M-1? Boy, they've sure improved the model from what we had when I was lugging one in Korea!" Harvey said. Burgle gurgled like a gallon jug of molasses suddenly up-ended and uncorked. Harvey assumed this was laughter.

"Youse can't fool me, buddy, but youse is sure a kidder! Good hypnocaster, hanh?" He did something to the watch, and shoved it under Harvey's nose again. This time, Harvey was a little surprised to see, it looked nothing like a watch. And now the dial read:

ENCEPHALOGRAPH, ELECTRO-
(MONODIRECTIONAL, MINIATURIZED)
Standard Galactic Empire Issue Model M-1

and right above this baffling inscription was a small plate flashing off and on with a red light. As Harvey watched, the blank plate blurred and letters formed upon it. They read: VEEBELFETZER TECHNICIAN.

A small, chill wind blew up Harvey's backbone. He cleared his throat of a sudden, lumpy obstruction that felt very much like his heart.

"That's . . . a very good trick," Harvey said weakly. "How'd you do it . . . ?"

"Trick?" Burgle rumbled. "Dat's da best hypnocaster *you* ever seen! Dey soaked me half a C-note fer it at Sirius Port!"

"Very good indeed," Harvey said, with a half-hearted attempt at a casual tone of voice. "Er . . . what exactly does an M-1 *do?*" Catching the gleam of suspicion in Burgle's eye, he added hastily: "I used to know but I forgot."

"Aww—cut de crap, willya?" Burgle scoffed, shrugging a pair of shoulders that should have belonged to a Mack truck. "Youse is still puttin' me on! De M-1 reads ya Alpha waves 'n' integrates 'em wid ya Beta levels, givin' a psycho-profile. *Youse* know *dat!*"

"Sort of an instant aptitude test, eh?" Harvey observed feebly. He wondered if he could make it back to the cab before this maniac went berserk. *Humor him, Harve ole boy,* he thought feverishly.

"*Sure!*" Burgle said, expansively. "*Dat's* how I spotted ya fer a veebelfetzer man! But I can't stan' around yakkin' all day, buddy, how's about signing up fer da *Queen o' Zarf,* hanh? Like I sez, we're short one hand on account of, see, our *ole* veebelfetzer tech ran inta a 'warp inna Coalsack and came out wid his *medulla oblongata* lookin' like a plate a scramble eggs. He ain't fit fer nuttin' but da funny farm, but lucky we hadda liddle psionic energy stored in duh mind-tanks and could set down here. Capt'n Grumbatz he sez, 'Burgle, get off ya can an go recruit us anudder veebelfetzer man, dis here planet, Oith, is crawlin' wid defectors, and if dey ain't at least one good veebelfetzer operator among de natives, we is stuck here till S Doradus freezes over!' So I checks da M-1 outa Ship's Stores an comes lookin'—so how's about it, bud?"

"Well," Harvey said with forced cordiality, "that

94

sure is a tempting offer. Mighty tempting. How *is* everything in the Space Patrol these days?"

"In da wha—? *Dis* is de Moichant Marine," Burgle snorted, with a certain dignity. He glared down at Harvey, then relaxed, permitting a genial grin to play over his hamburger of a face. He emitted another glottal chuckle, and slapped Harvey's back with a blow that nearly sent him head first into the wall of Krotzenheimer's.

"I get it, anudder gag! Jeez, youse sure are a card, bud!"

"Yean, a real joker," Harvey muttered, massaging his bruised shoulder. How was he going to get away from this lug?

"A—*joker*—I geddid! Oh, har har har. Dat's rich! I neveh knowed a fois'-rate veebelfetzer tech what dint have a fois'-rate sensa humor! So, anyway, how's about it, bud? Ship on da good ole *Queen o' Zarf* and see da univoice, hanh? How long sincet ya defectid? Not dat *we* cares," he added hastily, lowering his voice to a hoarse, conspiratorial whisper, "I mean, if youse is on de lam fer sumphin, youse got nuttin' ta feah. Da Moichant Marines neveh rats on a buddy. But, lissen, I ain't got time ta waste convoisin' all day—dis here planet is in a prohibited zone on accounta it's too primytive ta contact an if we gets caught hangin' around, it's da Big House fer evrybody. So, whadaya say, bud, hanh?"

"No . . . no thanks, pal," Harvey said with an attempt at breezy firmness. "See, I already got me a good job—it's parked at the curb over there—and, besides, well, I really *like* the Earth. I mean, I'm used to it by now—"

"Aww, c'mon, be a sport! Don't be like dat!

Whadaya wanna stick around dis crummy jernt fer? Dey call dis a civilization? Bet dey ain't a good ole-fashion Ovo-Snavery on de whole planet. An I bet youse couldn't get a snort o' Ole Space Ranger widin ten light-years!"

"Yeah, yeah, that's true, but I'm a bourbon man, myself," Harvey said. "And I rather like the placid unsullied peacefulness of this quiet backwater of galactic culture, what with its charmingly quaint and antique nuclear crises, fallout problems, test ban treaties, cold wars, air pollution index, Strontium 90 count, Communist infiltration into the Boy Scouts, and all. It's really a rest farm, after the hectic dog-eat-dog of the other planets in the galaxy . . ."

Burgle nodded, with little sympathetic grunts.

"I kin unnerstan' dat, bud, but—Jeez? I'd go bats if I wuz stuck in dis sleepy village more'n a week—" he gazed around scornfully at the Manhattan skyline where it thrust above the rows of Bronx apartments, "—an widout a Ovo-Snave, no tellin' what I'd do! How d'ya stand it?"

Harvey had been edging toward the alley mouth.

"Never touch the stuff, myself," he admitted absently, wondering if he should break and run, or what. "Just never got the habit, is all."

Burgle ogled him enviously. "Neveh? Jeez . . . I tried ta give 'em up ten, twenty times already, but I alweez went back ta—hey, where d'ya tink ya goin'—?" One hand the size of a medium Danish ham flashed out and caught Harvey by the upper arm. He felt himself lifted off the sidewalk and carried back into the dark alley again.

"Hey, look, Ugly, I don't mind a few laughs from a

trained ape, but watch it with the hands, okay?" He brushed Burgle's hand away and straightened his jacket. Adrenalin was pumping through his bloodstream, and he was getting mad. Besides, it had suddenly occurred to him he had no reason to fear this kooky gorilla. After àll, hadn't he been taking that mail-order course in karate, judo, and other Oriental Sciences of Self-Defense for the past two years? After all the dough he'd pumped down the drain for the course, he should be able to handle his weight in wildcats by now!

"Okay, okay, don't get boined up," Burgle muttered. "Jeez, all I'm tryin' ta do is sign ya up fer a trip ta Antares—big pay—eggzotic far-off places—booze, wimmen—da woiks! Come on—say 'oke'—don't make me hafta get tough—"

Harvey fell into his karate stance, half-crouched, one foot forward, one foot behind, right arm bent in front of his face.

"If anybody gets tough around here, ape-face, it'll be me! Now you just toddle along and count your marbles, and let me get back to work, okay?"

Burgle sighed, heavily.

"If youse wants it rough, bud, den we does it rough—"

Harvey saw Burgle point one finger at him, sadly. There was a spurt of blue fire from the end of that finger, and Harvey keeled over into a pit of blackness. The last thought that flashed through his mind before his brain flickered out like an overloaded light bulb was a taunting memory of Finster S. Cosgrove, and the story "Shanghaied by the Star Fiends" —then all went dark.

HARVEY OPENED HIS EYES and stared blankly at the room. It was a cramped cubbyhole with a low ceiling and two bunks, in one of which he was now lying. Beside the glaring light in the ceiling, he could see the grill of air-vent from which, together with a rattling noise of whirring fans, a flow of stale air came to his nostrils, heavily laden with the scents of machine oil and a particularly rank disinfectant. His head felt as if a troop of gremlins wearing iron boots were conducting a square dance on the surface of his cortex. He groaned and turned over.

This altered his field of vision, and brought a new sight hoving into his ken. Namely, an upright multi-legged thing covered with pebbly scarlet chitin. Its upper set of legs bore monstrous claws and from what he blurrily assumed was the creature's "head" he could see bright, inquisitive eyes examining him with alert interest. Unfortunately for his peace of mind, these eyes were not firmly set into a face, but extended about two feet from the head on branching stalks.

Harvey shut his eyes quickly. *I'm in a hospital and they've shot me full of morphine because of the unendurable pain of my hideous injuries,* he thought to himself. *Poor bastard, I'm out of my coconut,* he concluded.

Without opening his eyes, Harvey said weakly: "Did anybody get the number of that General Sherman tank that hit me?"

"Blimey, mate, you a blinkin' comedian or somethin'?" a nasal, droning voice with a pronounced Cockney accent said, from about two feet in front of him. "Yer okay now, don't try to fool *me*. Let's hop it —up to the Purser's hole and sign the bloody book— and look alive!"

Harvey opened one eye, and emitted a hollow groan. The thing was still there, scarlet eye-stalks and all. Only now he saw it was smoking a big green cigar. He squinched both eyes shut.

"B-better give me a shot that'll put me out, Doc, I'm having hallucinations!" he said feebly.

"I'll give yer a hallucination, mate, right at the end o' yer bloody nose in a minute, if you don't pop off that bunk and get hopping!" the creature snarled, rasping one huge claw angrily.

Harvey opened his eyes and, this time, held them open firmly, fighting against the impulse to curl into a fetal position and stay that way until everything went away.

"Gor blimey, mate, you off yer rocker, or what? You look like yer never saw an Arcturian lobster-man before—Lor' luvva duck if yer don't!"

"Well, as a matter of fact—since you bring the question up—*aaarrgghhh!*" Harvey, who had just sat up with his feet on the deck, suddenly felt his head split apart and then bang back together deafeningly, the two halves crashing like a couple of unlatched screen doors in a violent wind-storm. He reached up and tentatively felt with trembling hands. To his surprise, everything was still in one piece upstairs. And the rest of him seemed to work pretty well. Then why did he feel like two dozen jalopies were holding a drag race inside his skull? He groaned.

The Cockney lobster-man grated his mandibles together, in what may have been the Arcturian equivalent of a nasty snigger.

"Head ache, eh, matey? Too bloody bad—I *don't* think! Resistin' a press-gang ain't never smart. Ole Burgle had to let yew have it on the noggin with a neuronic stunner."

"Is that what it was?" Harvey mumbled, massaging his temples gingerly. "I could have sworn it was a General Sherman tank . . . and, not to strive for originality or anything, but—where the hell am *I*, anyway?"

"Lor' lumme, kid, where the blinkin' hell d'you *think* you are? Aboard the good ship *Queen o' Zarf*, that's where. Now, look alive, matey, and hop it up to the Purser's office and sign the book, will ya please? There's a luv!"

Harvey allowed himself to be pried off the bunk and stood, tottering a little, on his feet. Standing up, he was a bit relieved to see that the lobster-man only came up to his chest. Whether it was this slight psychological advantage, or the improved circulation effected by his erect posture, the drag race behind his forehead began to quiet down to a modest thumping.

"Kidnaping is one of the crimes still punishable by a death sentence," he said, pleasantly, "but I won't lodge a complaint with the authorities if you'll just—"

"Arr, none o' yer bleedin' lip to the likes o' *me*, I'll have yer know, mate. I'm Querziph, the Bos'un on this rusty ole tub, an' don't yer ferget it! Now hop along before I lose me temper and pin one on yer!"

A scarlet claw sizeable enough, and probably sharp enough, to snap through the Atlantic Cable, propelled Harvey out of the fo'c'sle into a narrow corridor. He came to a dead halt, gaping at a plastic screen set in the outer hull. There, against a coal-black backdrop thickly sprinkled with tiny points of

light, a huge bluish globe floated, flecked all over
with fuzzy patches of dim whiteness. He goggled.

"*Gahh!* Wh-what's that?"

The Bos'un fumed. "Oh, me Great Aunt Tilly,
whaddayer *think* it is, lovey? It Earth—Sol III—what
else? The ole *Queen* had just enough juice in her
tanks to give us a lift into orbit. Now you pop down
this way to the Purser and then get below to yer vee-
belfetzers—report to Chief Grumphzog—we're already
two ruddy, blinkin' days behind schedule, and this
load of zaylies an' garbers won't keep. The quicker
we dump 'em off at Tau Ceti, the happier the Old
Man'll be. *Git* along, now, there's a love."

There was nothing else to do. So Harvey stumbled
down the curving corridor in the direction Querziph
had pointed out (unnervingly, with an extensible
eye-stalk) and came to a halt, finally, before a door
that said: PURSER'S OFFICE. He started to knock
—realized he'd probably skin his knuckles, as the door
was a sheet of steel—reached for the handle—realized
there *was* no handle—and was thinking of giving up
and going back to resume that fetal position, when an
impatient voice from within, said crisply: "Going to
take all day? In with you, my lad, and be quick about
it!"

The door receded before his out-stretched fingers,
and Harvey entered—stumbling over the high sill. His
headache had been replaced with a queasy feeling,
once he realized he had been shanghaied aboard a
ship. He felt as if he might very well be sea sick any
minute . . . or would it be *space* sick? Helluva time
to be worrying about a question of nomenclature! He
looked around the crowded little office—and squeezed
his eyes shut, hurriedly.

101

"Come, come, haven't got all day! Stop making faces—there's a stout fella. Look like you've never seen a Cassiopian before!" the occupant of the small, very littered desk said in clipped British tones.

"Well . . . to be perfectly frank . . ."

"Here we go, then, there's a lad. *Name*."

Harvey opened his eyes. Hell, this one wasn't half as bad as the lobster-man with the green cigar! He looked rather like David Niven, if you could ignore the plum-purple skin, bright orange eyes, and startlingly white up-standing crest of feathery hair. He even had a little toothbrush mustache like David Niven—of white feathers, though. He certainly *sounded* like David Niven, Harvey thought, forgetting about the queasiness. Now there's a thought: how come all these extraterrestrials—if they *were* extraterrestrials, and Harvey was beginning to suspect, sickeningly, that they *were*—how come they all spoke with distinctively familiar terrestrial ethnic accents? Come to think of it, by God, how come they all spoke English anyway? Just what the merry hell was going on, anyway?

"I said, '*Name*'," the Cassiopian observed, frostily.

"Hodges, Harvey Arthur," Harvey said automatically. "Look here, I demand to speak to the American ambassador—you've no right to—"

"Age?" the purple-skinned version of David Niven inquired.

"38. And you can add 'Male, Caucasian, Unwed,' as well. I want to speak to the Captain—I want to call my lawyer—you—"

"Planet-of-birth?" the Purser continued, with true British imperturbability.

"*Earth*, damn it, that's what I've been—"

The Cassiopian speared him with a gimlet glance.

"Come, come, my dear fella, this simply won't do, you know! Earth is a primitive place, all very well if you like that sort of thing, but, well, frankly, *rather* low on the old technology-scale, what? Scarcely into the nuclear motive power phase, and still thousands of years from developing the veebelfetzer drive. So, a fine veebelfetzer operator like yourself could *hardly* come from such a backwards area."

"*But—!*"

The Purser silenced him with a lifted purple palm.

"Say no more. Not a word. My dear chap, I *quite* undertand. After all, you're hardly the *first* Imperial citizen to defect, to go 'native,' as the travelogues have it. Many of us feel the urge to break out of the same old rut, the humdrum job, the unhappy triune-marriage,—and some of us *do*. And what better way to avoid the hazards and obligations of citizenship in the Galactic Empire, than to settle down in a small, sleepy native village on a pre-Contact world—eh?"

"*I* didn't—!"

"Or," the calm voice overrode his anguished plaint smoothly, "if one has chanced to run afoul of some silly law or regulation—eh?—how better to avoid the messy business of a nasty arrest and trial and all that blather—than by hopping off to a sylvan retreat, like Earth, that (happily!) is part of a pro*hib*ited area, and thus well beyond Imperial jurisdiction? Eh? Quite."

"Quite," Harvey echoed, hollowly. "But don't you see—"

"But!" the Purser said, his voice ringing heartily, "*we* aren't the Space Patrol, after, all, are we now? Hmm? *This* is the maritime service, and, quite frankly, we're going to wink at the regulations just this once. *So* I shan't ask your real planet of birth—I'll just put down—hmm—Arcturus IV will do nicely—and I shan't ask to see your ID or even your papers—nor shall I put down the registry number of the last ship you veebelfetzed on—we'll just pick some numbers at random, from the air, as it were, heh? Quite!"

"Oh, quite," Harvey said, wearily.

"There, then, we're all set? Now—*do* be a good chap—pop right along to the engine room, third door to your left and down two decks—and report to the Chief for duty, eh?"

HARVEY HODGES was a simple, ordinary person, with a simple, ordinary character, and had enjoyed (up to now) what could well be described as a simple, ordinary life. A very unexciting and unglamorous life. The most exciting thing that had (up to now) ever happened to him, was being drafted during the Korean War. But even that had turned out to be unexciting, for Harvey had gone straight into the motor pool of a regimental headquarters company in a rear area, and had driven jeeps and three-quarter-ton trucks around for eleven months before his points were added up and he had been allowed to rotate home.

Out of the army, it just seemed natural for him, what with his excellent experience in the motor pool and all, to drift into a job driving a taxi for the Acme-All American Cab Company. It was a job like any other job he could have gotten. Not very exciting, of course, but plenty of security, three squares a day and enough dough left over for two weeks in Atlantic City every summer. It was a living.

To inject a little excitement, even if it was only of the synthetic variety, Harvey read science fiction magazines. And after laying down the latest *Weird Scientific Thriller Monthly* or *Cataclysmic Science Adventures,* he would often, of a lazy Saturday afternoon, stare dreamily at the ceiling of his room in Mrs. Hufferd's apartment house on West 92nd Street, and picture himself as the hero of one of the yarns he had been reading. Lots of the stories were about an "ordinary Joe"—generally either an ace test-pilot, or a Federal agent, or (at the very least) a crack reporter for the *Daily Comet*—from here and now, who gets embroiled in a fantastic adventure zipping about through space and/or time. Sometimes it was a square-jawed young archeologist who digs up an Underground World. Or a daredevil pilot who gets caught up in a Flying Saucer. Or a broad-shouldered nuclear physicist who presses the wrong stud and is catapulted into the Fourth Dimension.

He'd *never* read one yet, in which a dopey cab-driver pushing forty gets shanghaied onto a "tramp spacer" or whatever, and carried off into the farthest reaches of Galactic Space.

And besides. All the guys in the stories were always at least six foot three and built like Rock Hudson used to be. And had engineering training that would make Einstein gasp, and could (when cornered) pilot a space ship or weld forty-seven busbars together into a super nucleo-electronic gamma tightbeam disintegrator.

Harvey didn't have the foggiest notion of how to pilot a space ship. Much less, operate a veebelfetzer. He didn't even know what a veebelfetzer *was,* for gosh sakes. But nobody would listen to him! Well, by golly, they'd damn sure have to listen when they strapped him into the veebelfetzer machine and put the electrodes against his skull (or whatever it was you did to operate a veebelfetzer)—and *nothing happened*. THEN they'd listen to him, by God, and put him back on Earth quick enough, prohibited area or no—

These thoughts, or a perhaps somewhat less rational equivalent thereof, had been churning through Harvey's head while he made his way down to the engine room—when suddenly it struck him.

Oh-oh.

He stopped dead—ah, motionless, please. Let's not be negative and think about being *dead*.

What, exactly, *would* they do when they strapped him into the veebelfetzer and screwed the jolly old electrodes on his temples—and then found it was all a ghastly mistake, and he couldn't veebelfetz worth a hounddog's hoot?

Found, in point of fact, he was *not* a defector fleeing from the hectic complexities of modern galactic civilization at all—but just a simple, ordinary Earthling? Eh?

Call the Space Patrol and say: "Golly, we're sorry about this, but we landed in this prohibited area, the Earth, in *total, cold-blooded and calculated defiance of Imperial Law and kidnaped this helpless, dopey Earthling by knocking him cross-eyed with a neuronic stunner* and, gee, we're sorry and we won't ever do it again, fellows, so now let's let him loose on Earth to tell the whole world about the Galactic Empire."

Yeah, *sure*.

Sure that's what they'd do—in a pig's ear!

Harvey allowed himself the luxury of a small, bitter

106

smile. He knew what they'd do—knock him on the head and chuck him out the nearest airlock, *that's what!* Hadn't Burgle said something about illegal Contact with a prohibited area? Some thing about "lock us all up in the Big House for twenty years" or some-such phrase?

Cold sweat dewed Harvey's brow.

What the hell was he going to do?

How could he delay being strapped in the bloody old veebelfetzer for the acid test? What would one of the heroes in a science fiction story do?

"Bluff, that's it, Harve ole boy, sheer bluff," he muttered to himself, continuing on down the stair. "Stiff upper lip, as that purple limey upstairs would say. Never let the swine know they've got you worried! Head bloodied but unbowed, that's the trick, and when Chief what-zis-name's back is turned, tossa monkey wrench into the veebelfetzer and look innocent, no matter what the—*wow!*"

"Vot's midt you, nutty? Vot's midt der talkin' to yourself, iss you der kook, or vot?"

A door marked ENGINE ROOM had popped open before him and a nine-foot-high grizzly bear, pea-soup-green from head to toe—err—*claw*—stood glaring at him and chewing on a stogie. He wore oil-stained overalls and had a huge wrench sticking out of his—it's—rear pocket.

Never let 'em know they've got you rattled; cool as a cucumber now.

"Ah, there, sorry, you startled me for a moment. Chief Grumphzog, I believe?" Harvey said glibly, with a bright smile. The shaggy green grizzly bear looked him over sourly, and didn't seem to like what he saw.

107

"Undt who *else* vould I be, dumkopf? Vot you been doingk, hey? You valk here on der hands undt knees, or vot? Gott in himmel, I haff seen veebelfetzer men in my time, but I svear dey gedt crummier effery year. Come in, come in, you tink ve vant to sidt in orbidt all 'day vaitink on you?"

"Quite right, sorry about that, new to the ship and all, ha ha," Harvey said, inching past the towering monster into the engine room. Fantastic machinery of totally unfamiliar design loomed in the dim light of a few bulbs to either hand. Brass glittered dully, and the steel deck underfoot was stained with oil. Grumbling something in gruff German, the Chief Engineer slammed the door shut behind them.

Harvey glanced around despairingly, then, catching the green grizzly bear's sour eye, laughed heartily.

"Now, don't say it, Chief! I'll bet you think I've never seen a Betelgeusean bear-man before, right?"

"Vot you say dere, you crazy midt der head or vot? Dere is only *vasp*-men midt der Betelgeusers, dumkopf!"

"Ha, ha, wasp-men to be sure, how silly of me!"

"Crazy veebelfetzer gestunkener! I'm dere bearman from der *Fomalhaut* . . . Gott in himmel, crazier effery year, dese veebelfetzeren!"

"Simple mistake, ha ha," Harvey laughed hollowly. "Well, well, so *this* is the engine room. My, my," he said, gazing around admiringly, "look at all the—er—engines!" His gaze lighted on one particularly fantastic mechanism, a left-over prop from Dr. Frankenstein's laboratory, perhaps, looking rather like the ill-gotten offspring of an operating table and several dozen yards of neon tubing.

"Ah, and here we have the good old veebelfetzer

108

machine, I'd say! Fine looking instrument, Chief, really fine—"

"So uff course dis is der veebelfetzer machine, crazy-head, vot else?"

Rather disconcerted, Harvey recoiled. "It is?" He eyed the grim flat table apprehensively, noting carefully the heavy straps for wrists, ankles and waist. "By golly, if this was Transylvania, I'd say you were all set up to transplant some brains down here, Chief—"

"Vot der crazy-talk—?"

"Never mind, pay no attention," Harvey said, distractedly. *Toss a monkey wrench in the works, that's the old trickeroo!* "Let me borrow that spanner I see sticking out of the back pocket of your jeans, Chief, thanks. A few adjustments needed—oh, don't mind if I babble on like this, it's nothing, always a bit nervous before I—ah—veebelfetz, you know. *Say!*" he broke off as a sudden flash of inspiration galvanized him. *Distract the bugger while I blow up the gizmo,* he thought.

The Chief jumped nervously.

"Vot?"

"How're you fixed for frammistan coils? Got enough, I hope?"

"Ya, ya, ve haff a whole locker-full," the Chief rumbled, turning to wave one vast green paw at a distant corner of the room. While his back was turned, Harvey rammed the wrench into an unobtrusive portion of the veebelfetzer, picking an outstandingly vulnerable-looking tangle of electronic ganglia. *That'll hold you, buster,* he thought with gritted teeth.

As the Chief turned back, Harvey rubbed his hands together and flashed a winning smile.

"Well, I'm all set if you are, Chief! That's right, let's

strap me into the veebelfetzer . . . ah, that's the trick
. . . gad! it seems like *ages* since I was last strapped
into the good old veebel—good Christ, you really *do*
screw electrodes to my temples, eh, Chief?—ah, there
we are!"

Chief Engineer Grumphzog tightened a last strap
and stepped back to survey his handiwork. "Hey, crazy-head, iss dot all right?" he inquired. Harvey turned
a face like a death's-head towards him, paper-white,
lips stretched back in a maniacal grin, sweat glinting
slickly from brow and cheeks.

"Comfy, right comfy," he said. "Turn on the juice,
Warden, and say goodbye to Mom for me. I swear
you're fryin' an innocent man, but maybe the Gover-
nor'll come through with that good ole reprieve.
Never say die, is my motto."

Shaking his head and muttering, "Crazy-talking all
der time, dis no-good veebelfetzer!" the Chief ambled
over to the control console and switched on the inter-
com with one green paw.

"Enchine room to der bridge. Mein Kapitan! Ve iss
all set down here, der crazy-talkin' veebelfetzer undt
I. Ya, ya, I undterstandt. Hokay." He switched off the
set and turned a stern glance on the helpless form
strapped into the machine.

"Hey, crazy-head," he boomed. "Vatch for der
green light undt ven you see it, *veebelfetz!* Got dat?"

Here we go into sub-space, or what-you-will,
Harvey thought. *How do I get into things like this?
Oh-oh, there's the good old green light! Ready—set—
VEEBELFETZ, YOU BUM! Monkey wrench, do
your work!*

The green light went off and Harvey watched, with
what inward trepidation I give my reader liberty to

imagine, as the burly, shaggy figure of Chief Grumph-zog left the controls and ambled purposefully toward his helpless form. Since the Chief's head was bushy, prick-eared, and muzzled like a grizzly, it was impossible to read any expression that might be inscribed thereupon. Harvey grinned with the false elation of near-hysteria.

The moment of truth, he thought, as the Chief extended massive paws toward him, hooked, he now noticed, with curving claws that ought to be great at a party with lots of beer cans around.

"Well, what's the verdict, Chief, a blaster-bolt between the eyes, or am I just going to get shoved out of the nearest air-lock without spacesuit—" he broke off, baffled. The Chief was making a curious sound, deep in his barrel-chest.

He was *chuckling!*

"You okay, Chief?"

. The Chief cuffed him affectionately with one soft paw, and helped him up off the table. "*Vot* a veebel-fetzer! Mein poy, neffer haff I seen dose needles jump like dot before, neffer!"

Tottering on knees that threatened to fold in several different directions at once, Harvey regarded him suspiciously. "You okay, Chief? Didn't pop a gasket, or something?"

"*Vot* power! *Vot* control! *Vot* apilidy! Mein poy, I am tellink you, you are ein very *brince* of veebelfetz-ers—"

Harvey's voice went all squeaky.

"You mean *I VEEBELFETZED?*"

"Did *you* veebelfetz—ho poy! Ten boindt fife light years like it voss nodingk! *Poof.* Now ve godt maybe ten, twelve hours cruisingk on conwentional drive

111

undt den ve landt at Tau Ceti undt unload all doss gestunkener gerbers undt zayhes *undt* make a tidy brophet *undt* ve iss two days ahead schedule, nodt behindt."

"Ten . . . point . . . five . . . light years, you said." Harvey gulped, grew (if possible) even paler, then flushed as color drained back into his face and took a deep breath.

"Great Gernsback, I can do it!"

"Yah, yah, you can do it, mein poy. *Such* a veebelfetzer, I neffer saw, undt truth I am tellingk you."

"Hey, Mom, I'm a veebelfetzer. Hot damn," Harvey said, weakly. "Burgle was right. The good ole M-1 was on the beam after all! Whatever it is, I can do it . . ."

"Yah, mein poy, now no more crazy-talkingk. You gedt back to das fo'castle undt take ein liddle nap now, dere's a goodt poy, ve don't need you vor avile."

But Harvey wasn't listening.

Harvey was out cold, smiling like an angel.

❋

SO, WELL, that's how it started. You know? I figgered, Jeez, I got this great talent for veebelfetzing . . . so, what the hell, why should I raise a stink about bein' shanghaied an' all? What was I doin' back on Earth but driving a lousy hack. So what's so great about being a hackey? And how's it any different, hacking, from veebelfetzing a spaceship around?

Well, you know, it wasn't.

So I veebelfetzed. For two years I veebelfetzed. We hit every damn port between here and the Lesser Magelanic, and I gotta admit Captain Grumbatz paid good for quality veebelfetzing and I stacked up a real pile of the jolly old credits. Trouble was, you see, I get itchy fingers for the old schnicklefritz. The roulette wheel, we'd call it back home. Fast as the loot piled up, I'd shovel it out into the graspin' claws of the croupiers.

And then, along come this new-fangled whatzit. Some bloody scientist—they oughta pass a law against them bums, I tell ya!—first thing I know, some wisenheimer up an invents this here Geheimerschtatzer Drive . . .

And where does that leave ol' Harve, I ask ya? Out in the cold, that's where. *Bang, zot,* like that, I git bounced outa my job. The crumbums. What? Well, that rusty old tub, the *Queen o' Zarf,* the owners convert her ta Geheimerschtatzers, and where does that leave a good, hard-workin' veebelfetzer man? On th' beach, that's where . . .

Oh, you gotta go! Well, lissen now, it's been real great jawin' with ya, and an I wanna thank ya for the caffeine-derivative and them sandwiches, an . . .

Ah, shucks. You dint hafta go and do *that.* Well, sure, I could certainly use a coupla creds, but a whole dang C-note? Lissen, I'm no *bum,* ya know! I don't hafta take no charity from nobody, I gotta Skill, I got —I gotta *Career . . .*

Well, then, okay. But just as a loan, you know? Pay you back just as soon as I get me another job. Why, hell, I hear that freighter headin' out for Groomsbridge 31184 oughta be in any day now, and it's a old tub, ya know: one they ain't converted to those lousy, stinkin', no-good Geheimerschtatzers yet, and I hear they need a good veebelfetzer man aboard . . . why, shucks, I'm still good enough to push that tub half-

113

way to Andromeda an' back without even blowing a fuse . . .

So, thanks a lot, and I don't mind taking the dough. But just as a loan, okay? Just till I land that job; just till the ship gets in. Okay. And I'll be payin' ya back *real* soon.

Any day now.

❀

Hmmm. Maybe it really *should* have been a novel . . . I see I left a couple loose plot-threads dangling, like how come the e.t.'s speak ethnic English . . . oh, well.

❀

I REMEMBER writing this next story one afternoon in 1965. It kept me at the old IBM Electric Model B most of the evening as well. It is a strange little yarn, told in a style very different from my usual, and I was enormously relieved when Avram Davidson liked it and bought it for *The Magazine of Fantasy and Science Fiction,* because I had deep doubts about it myself, it was so un-Carterian. Oddly, it turned out to be my most successful short story ever. After the magazine printing, it was snapped up by an anthology (*World's Best Science Fiction: 1966,* the first of the annual Ace anthologies), and it has since gone into an Italian translation, etc. I hope it grabs you, too . . .

❀

UNCOLLECTED WORKS

STRANGE THAT you should ask if I minded growing old! Actually, old age has much occupied my mind recently. Age, you see, my boy, has overtaken me by such imperceptible degrees that I was hardly conscious of its surreptitious advance. But, of late, I have had the matter brought to my attention by a certain shortness of breath and an increased and unsteady activity of my heart, whenever I am foolish enough, or forgetful enough, to climb stairs or to walk further along the cliffs than I have been accustomed to doing.

Age is a curious phenomenon, if I may call it that (for I would rather, for my peace of mind, rank it with the accidents than with the certainties of life). Its symptoms in my case, save for certain minor physical annoyances, such as those already alluded to, are rather pleasantly limited to a lack of—what shall I call

115

it?—excitability, perhaps? At any rate, the brave, burning issues of literature, which, in my more youthful years, seemed so desperately important, can now scarcely rouse me to anything stronger than a vague displeasure, or, pleasure. I find I have become more interested in the temperature of my afternoon tea than in the current state of letters; more concerned with the health of my El Martinique roses than with the decline in elegance of form . . . all subjects which once aroused within my bosom a degree of fervor and evangelical zeal I am now mildly embarrassed to recollect.

The life of a literary critic (or, as I much prefer to entitle my 'calling,' an *apostle of letters*) does, after all, seldom demand violent physical activity or emotional exertion. Therefore I am hardly made aware of any lessening of my bodily or my intellectual capabilities. As for life itself . . . you know, young man, when I look back on my little handful of years, I find it oddly difficult to disentangle the strands of my personal life from the texture of my literary career. Does that disturb you or make you feel sorry for an aging *enfant terrible?* But it is true: I cannot be sure, for example, which has enraged or distressed me more in recent years, the death of my third wife, a lovely child, or the lamentable stupidity of the Swedish Academy of Literature in failing to award the Nobel accolade to the great, the gigantic Ezra Pound before his death last year made it forever impossible for him to reject the prize, as doubtless he would have done, and with enormous glee (alas, he always swore he would outlive me by at least enough time wherein to compose a savage epitaph for my obituary: I loved the man for his brilliant work, but I fear I attacked too fiercely his terminal volume of *canzoni*). And I find myself, when looking backward on them, dating the inner crises of my emotional/personal life by the calendar events of my public career . . . "When did I meet Par Lagerkvist?" I will ask myself. "Ah, yes, that summer Solange and I rented the blue villa near Capri!" Or: "Now, where *was* I living when Roger was born?" "Of course, it was when I was busy correcting proofs on my *Filigree*, so I must have been in Paris."

(Does all of this seem inhumane—or inhuman—to you, young man? Well, perhaps it is. Who was it—Bertrand Russell?—who once, and rightly, observed, "books make a damned poor substitute for living." I fear I am the incarnate proof of that well-coined adage, although I could make the reply, "yes, but life is damned dreary without books.")

What did you say? Ah, you have read *Filigree*, eh? Well, it was an amusing little trifle, an experiment with form, little more, and it beguiled me in the making all one lovely summer. You know, it is a distinct pleasure to discover that an occasional young journalist like yourself actually *reads* something of the authors he makes up features about! And, yes, I am touched and pleased to learn that at least one of my little books is still alive among the young, that the young people still remember me; for you might say that it is my greatest regret in life that I was not gifted by the Gods to be a creator of genuine literature myself, but merely one of that lesser breed who merely comment, in print, on the productions of superior genius. Yes, I confess myself flattered that you came all this way to gather "copy" on an old, neglected writer-upon-writers. I am surprised, in fact, that your magazine (I'm sorry to say I am not familiar with it, but we get so very few American periodicals on this side of the water), that your magazine, I say, should be at all interested in a passé gentleman of letters like myself, as they must be, to send you all this way for an interview. I hope, I *do* hope, that you will not ask for my opinions on Mr. William Burroughs and his work, or why I refused to attend that testimonial dinner for Robert Graves in London . . .

Eh? Is that my chief regret? Oh, probably not. I lack the, shall I say, *stamina* for genuinely creative work. Criticism takes much less out of one, you know. Literature demands a certain sheer physical durability, at least first-rate literature. Like Tom Wolfe scribbling his colossal novels on paper pads in illegible long-hand on top of his icebox, during forty-six-hour sessions. Or Hemingway living on gin and black coffee for days at a stretch, when in the throes of a novel. That sort of thing. Typewriter-pounding is hard work, young man, hard work indeed. Ditch-digging, by comparison, demands far less of one, or so I have been told by any number of ambitious young first-novelists who underwrote their apprentice years with day-labor.

What *is* my chief regret? Ah, that is an interesting question! I doubt if I should be fully honest. You might say my chief regret is never having met Yeats. Or that I later regretted having so savagely penned that satirical critique of Joyce's *Portrait of the Artist,* when it was being serialized in *The Egoist* in 1913 or whenever it was. But—no, that would be telling you what you and your readers would expect to hear from me; it would be begging the question. And it is not true at all . . .

Shall I be very cryptic, young man, yet utterly truthful? Very well: I most regret that I shall never live to read the supreme masterpiece of American fiction, Willard Paxton's *Those Who Err*. Or at least, I very much doubt if I shall still be around to read it, for it shall not be printed until some forty years from now. Long after I am dead and gone to Abram's bosom, which has always sounded to me like a rather intimate location to spend the afterlife in . . . forty years after I am dead, it will be published (if the local physicians are correct in their current estimates of my present state of durability).

Or, that I shall never taste the merciless wit of those glittering comedies that shall earn for the as-yet-unborn Juan Ramon Chiminez his immortality as "the Argentine Shakespeare" . . . or those intoxicating and intricate sonnets, *The Adorations*, which Claude de Montaubon shall not commit to print until seventy-six years have passed.

What else could you expect an aging critic to regret, but those masterpieces of the future as yet unwritten, whose very authors have not yet been born?

Bear with me, young man. And you need not look at me quite so askance . . . my wits are intact, I assure you, although my body may be somewhat the worse for wear. I know you could never dare publish what I am about to tell you—for I am going to be very foolish and tell you *the truth*. Something I have never revealed to anyone, not to a living soul. Bear with me, if you will . . . let a talkative and lonely old man unburden himself of a terrible secret, here, in the shadow of his summer roses . . .

*

I NEVER knew his name. To me, these many, many years, he has been simply: The Gentleman in Green. An enigma, a mystery, a puzzle *sans* solution, a riddle that has never been answered, like Lewis Carroll's "Why is a raven like a writing-desk?"—except that I once conceived of an answer to that time-honored baffler: "Because Poe wrote on *ḅoth*" . . .

Sometimes I have wondered if I ever met him at all, in reality; in what we choose, rather arbitrarily, to consider reality. Perhaps his tall figure slipped into my life from a waking dream, perhaps he was a phantom of the mind, dreamed in a doze over a cool glass of good Medoc on a soft and wistful autumn afternoon . . .

Do you know Paris? Ah, if you know Paris at all, you must know the Left Bank. There is a certain little cobbled side-street off the Place d'Opera that meanders up the hills toward the old Cathedral. Many years ago there was a tiny, and very dirty, *bistro* on that crooked little street that wanders and zigzags its shabby and dilapidated way under the shadow of Bernette's bell-tower, once the talk of the Continent, with its corbeled arches and baroque sexless angels, and pigeons roosting on their blown, frozen bronze tresses. Nearby lay the attic studio where Nerval once lived, and down the hill toward the Opera, that stucco apartment building whose *concierge,* if persuaded with a coin or two, could wheeze out some quaint anecdota concerning d'Auberville and the poets of the Paladins, who used to gather there on rainy Proustian afternoons and utter manifestoes designed to resuscitate the Gallic muse.

I had scarcely been a month in Paris. The unexpected success (critical, that is, not monetary) of my first slim volume of verse had gone to my head. *Man dragore*, I called it, and its triumph would, I assumed, soon waft me to fame as a coming young poet. Still lacking of twenty, I fled the bourgeois, stifling atmosphere of America, hoping to find in the City of Light those ideal and paradisical regions in whose pure, stimulating atmosphere "perfect verse" could be composed, and among whose aloof, imperious and Olympian *salons* I would take my brilliant place. Ah—to be young, and a poet, and to live in Paris in those dim, dead days! It was Valhalla and El Dorado combined, that city where Proust drowsed and Heine starved. An industrious young Degas labored in every garret, and several wilted Rimbauds still ornamented the more picturesque gutters and scrawled *Dieu est mortel* on alley-walls with pastel chalks. Oh, dear God, but I was young . . .

I had spent a fatiguing day. Two editors I had bearded in their dens, in fear and trembling but *sans* result. The future of modern verse I had argued out with a bearded expatriate Russian who resembled an unkempt goat and rather smelled like one, and who vehemently persevered in holding the obstinant opinion, which seemed to me nonsensical, that the direction of verse lay in *vers libre* imitations of Pushkin.

I stopped on my way back to my flat, pausing at the little bistro for a cool glass and a warm bun. It was crowded with sightseers en route to or from the Cathedral, so I shared a corner table with an elderly gentleman of scholarly and even professorial appearance. He was neatly but cheaply dressed, slim and going gray over the temples; he wore an old suit of bottle-green corduroy, with a loose *foulard* at his throat, half-hidden behind a sharp little spike of a

Napoleon III goatee. It is a universal custom that any two strangers forced to share a table ignore each other, and thus did we, save for a covert sidewise glance or two. He sat back, idly sipping a Pernod, watching the crowd. When next he reached for his glass I noticed his hands. They were stained with black oily grease: the hands of a mechanic. But, no, when I looked more closely, I saw that the grease was no mere oily lubricant but expensive graphite used to facilitate the workings of the most delicate gears. A watchmaker, perhaps? I decided not. Something about him savored of the basement inventor, while his long hair and the genteel decay of his accouterments suggested the artist.

His face was in shadow, but his profile, with the jutting small pointed beard and the patriarchal, hawk-beaked nose, inescapably reminded me of El Greco's portrait of Cardinal Giambatiste in the Louvre.

My curiosity ebbed. My attention wandered. I sat back and drew out a copy of my book and leafed through it. I fear I was so enthralled with my new-born authorship that I carried *Mandragore* everywhere with me, and carelessly drew it out to read pointedly in public.

The *garçon* brought my drink and my companion finished his. Somehow or other, with the bustling, busy waiter as a pretext, the two of us struck up a conversation. I was proud to display what I fancied to be an exquisite command of aristocratic French; scorning as a lowly *touriste* the loutish American who speaks only English in Paris, I flaunted my linguistic accomplishments at every opportunity. He elicited from me my profession, seemed impressed at my status, and confessed his assumption that I was but another student. In our exchange, the stranger casually exercised a remarkable and unorthodox literary knowledge which excited my interest. I overrode his polite protest and bought him a Pernod—I was drinking Medoc, a good vintage, and priding myself on the taste of a born connoisseur. Our drinks came, and I listened as he began talking.

"As you may have noticed from the disreputable condition of my hands, young sir, I am a mechanical technician. In fact, if you will permit, something of an inventor in a modest way. I am fortunate enough to possess a few small patents, idly obtained in my industrious youth, and these fetch an income sufficient for my simple needs. So I can live as I please and continue my experiments as I wish."

At this point I inquired as to his branch or specialty. He replied: "Alas, the proper term has yet to be coined! But for my own amusement, I have christened the area of my interests by the unlikely name of *bibliochanics*.

When I was a young student in Prague I studied under Gouffé, then famous as 'the Genius of the Machine.' This was long before you were born, or even conceived, I am sure. I read widely and, I fear, indiscriminately in those student years. I recall an image, a metaphor, a paradox, call it what you will—something in one of the philosophers which so intrigued my mind and stimulated the curiosity of the young intellectual I then was, that it became a profound and motivating force on my future career. Perhaps you have already encountered the concept: it suggested that if you were to employ fifty million monkeys, scribbling aimlessly (this was long before the typewriter became popular, of course), they would eventually and in the fullness of time, reproduce the works of Montaigne, complete and letter-perfect, to the last dot of an *i* and crossing of a *t*."

I nodded. I had somewhere encountered the same idea, or a paraphrase of it: in my day, the it had been "the complete works of Shakespeare," but I let it pass without comment, curious as to where all this was leading—as, perhaps, are you.

He adjusted a monocle, sipped his drink, and continued:

"I was *possessed* by that paradox. The verb is precisely apt: it was as if an evil spirit had entered into me, and seized control of my person. The idea enchanted and fascinated me: I speculated endlessly over it. Later, in my courses of mathematics and symbolic logic at the University, I was literally electrified to discover that even so quaint and bizarre a concept was, after all, well within the bounds of the credible. For the total number of possible combinations of letters in any language is quite finite, I learned. Of course, at a liberal guess, it would take the fifty million monkeys about fifty thousand years to hit on Montaigne. But, still, it *was* possible.

"And so I became an experimental mechanical technician. And a highly successful one, if I may be so immodest as to admit the truth. During the years that followed, and they were busy ones and crowded with events, I remained under the power of that devilish and diabolical concept. At length, financially independent due to my facility for "tinkering," I began playing with the idea at earnest. And, again, the verb is precise, for I toyed with the concept as an idle amusement, curious to see how best the notion might

124

be translated into mechanical actuality. Such conceits were common in my time. Half the inventors of my acquaintance were eccentrics, with a perpetual-motion machine hidden away in the closet, or a fantastic and da Vincian aerofoil concealed in the attic. My hobby was a writing-machine.

"After some years of idle tinkering, I perceived of a means whereby the device might be made workable, and a leisurely hobby gave way to an absorbing period of mechanical design. What eventuated was not very unlike the modern typewriter, but perfected far beyond that crude device. It did not employ letters affixed to the ends of rods wherewith the platen could be struck, for such was too cumbersome and time-consuming a process. Instead, I devised wheels with raised letters set along the outer surfaces—wheels which revolved at random, creating a patternless meaninglessness—a chaos of pure Chance—numberless combinations of letters were thus printed and accumulated in a twinkling. Since I did not have fifty thousand years to spare on the project, my central and prime concern was to accelerate the accumulation of printed letter-combinations, so that the few years at my disposal should equal the vast number required. In endless experiments, I gradually refined my designs. My experiments devoured many years, and consumed my youth as well, but I worked on tirelessly. My writing-machine went through a hundred models, a hundred improvements, and its costs ate deeply into my small stipend. Luckily, I was able —purely as by-products to my main experiment—to patent several valuable modifications on the linotype and the typewriter, which provided the wherewithal to continue my work. Rather early in my attempts to increase the speed of the combinations, I eliminated actual letters as such, replacing them with spools of paper tape punched with a coded system of dots and dashes. Next, I invented a phonetic system composed of *sounds,* not letters at all—but I shall not bore you with a step-by-step account of the machine's development. Eventually, my machine was ready to—begin.

"I called it *Bibliac,* from the Greek *biblio* "book," and the admission that only a "maniac" would invent a device to simulate the random scrawlings of fifty million chimpanzees! My invention, by this stage, operated at amazing speed and compiled completely random combinations of letters, which I called *word-forms.* It 'wrote' at a speed impossible to achieve by hand. Its whirling wheels perforated code-combinations in spools of thick paper tape, simulating the actions of a typewriter, or many typewriters, but hundreds and even thousands of times faster than that antiquated device could duplicate. I had achieved ultimate speed by reducing both the size of the paper spools and the coded wheels, to the point where a single turn of a single wheel punctured *hundreds* of wordforms on the receptive tape, in endless variations.

"In short, I had the mechanical equivalent of fifty million monkeys. It filled half the upper floor of my house, and ran tirelessly, powered by a system of weights, balances, and springs."

"And did it produce Montaigne?" I asked. My tone must have been light, for the Gentleman in Green fixed me with a serious, even a stern, glance of reproof.

"No, it did not. For many months, in fact, *Bibliac*

126

produced endless and undiluted gibberish—at the rate of seventeen million 'words' a day, however."

"But surely you did not actually *read—?*"

"No. I had devised a Monitor that spot-scanned the tapes in random samplings, and was keyed to register any significant combination of phonemes—anything that suggested a logical or meaningful pattern. After two full years of this, during which my inexhaustible *Bibliac* continued to operate virtually without pause or rest, such a meaningful combination *was* noted! The Monitor reported that the wordforms were beginning to take on a semblance of coherent construction. I translated the coded tapes into recognizable letters, but could make no sense out of the wordforms at all. However, the pattern persisted. It was utter Babel, yet familiar constructions were irregularly repeated. It was undeniable that *Bibliac* had evolved a vocabulary of sorts: phonemic combinations—meaningless 'words'—were used over and over. Well, one cannot devote a sizeable portion of one's life to a project and give up without a struggle. In despair of making any sense out of *Bibliac*'s productions, I transcribed the first portions into the Roman alphabet and determined to secure the advice of an old friend from the University, who had made his home in Paris in his later years, even as had I. He identified the text without delay—why had I never thought to consult a *linguist!*

" 'Why, of course,' Markoy said when I showed him my transcription. 'You have here an early portion of *Enmerkar and the Lord of Aratta,* the ancient Babylonish epic. In the original Sumerian, too. It is, as you may be aware, widely considered *the most ancient known work in any literature . . .*"

"FROM THAT point on," continued the Gentleman in Green, "I dwelt in Paradise, tasting such delights as only he can savor, who sees his dream of a lifetime coming true before his eyes. *Bibliac* wrote on, producing the complete text of the Sumerian, the Akkadian, and the Babylonian literatures, the oldest known to man . . . and I was forced to realize that I had never thought about the logical implications inherent in the paradox of the fifty million monkeys . . . of course the hairy typists would not produce Montaigne out of a blue sky . . . naturally, they would have to work up to him, by duplicating the full literary tradition!

"Rapt in fascination, I tended my whirling, racketting machine, tending its needs with the finest lubricants money could purchase, poring enthralled over each day's literary productions. Ere long, *Bibliac* had progressed through the late Babylonians, the Assyrians, the Hittites, the ancient Egyptians, and was well into Homer. From that point on, of course, the results were predictable."

I gaped at him. "Can it be . . . you mean?"

My Gentleman in Green nodded with a faint smile. "The logical implications of the paradox . . . don't you see what the fifty million monkeys represent? Not a nonsense-symbol, but an historical reality. For there existed a living equivalent of the fifty million monkeys, *the human race itself*, whose literature began with that Sumerian epic and worked slowly upwards to the era of Montaigne!"

I stared at him, staggered, wondering whether he

were mad or merely entertaining me with a fanciful and amusing fable—but completely caught up in the fascination of his tale. He continued:

"I watched as *Bibliac* reproduced the entire literature of the Greeks (including the fourteen lost comedies of Aristotle which perished in the flames that consumed the Alexandrian Library, the long-vanished *Marsyas* of Homer, the books of the Cyclic poets, otherwise extant but in scattered fragments). By winter, *Bibliac* had gotten as far as the Romans. Before Christmas, the lost literature of the Carthaginians was regained—I kept it piled on a work-bench near the window, and amused myself with calculating what the professors of the Sorbonne would pay to have it in their hands!—and by spring we had entered into the Dark Ages: we would arrive at the Renaissance before Easter, which seemed most appropriate. I was watching the complete vindication of my life's work —the fulfillment of my dream!"

I ordered our glasses refilled, and as the long gray shadows of afternoon mingled with the plum-purple of evening, he talked on. He and *Bibliac* had worked through the dreary literary productions of the Reformation, he recalled, and thus into modernity. I lost the thread of his remarks for a bit—I must confess that I was secretly wondering if his amazing machine had reproduced the text of my *Mandragore*. But this I did not dare ask . . . I have often wondered about it, since.

"And now that *Bibliac* is silent," I interjected, "you must be ready to publish an account of your experiment in whatever scholarly journals devote their pages to the mechanistic science. You should reap a well-deserved harvest of fame—"

His reply was a quick glance of startled resentment.

"'Silent'?" he repeated blankly. "But it is not—the work goes on!"

"How can it go on, when it has already reached . . ."

"Already we are well past the literature of the 21st Century," he stated. *"Bibliac* is printing the unwritten works of the future!"

The stunning shock his words created must have been visibly traced on my features, for he leaned forward, tapping the tabletop with a lean forefinger for emphasis.

"Listen to me, young man! I have perused the works of genius that shall not be penned till long after you and I are dust. I have pondered the poems which will astonish the world in the age of your grandchildren. That gigantic novel, *Those Who Err,* whose author, Willard Paxton, will die before completing it, even as did the great Cervantes, leaving unfinished his masterpiece, the *Quixote,* to which Paxton's novel will often be compared! And I have read the *Arthuriad* of Gwyn Rhys Jones—a Welshman and the greatest epic poet since Milton. And I have explored the intricate music of the cyclic-dramas of Von Bremen, and the rich dream-imagery of *Taliesin in Limbo,* for which the English King Charles IV will knight Edward Quinsey Marlinson. I alone of all men in the world, recall the subtle cadences of the opening couplet of Tierney's great mock-romance, *Baghdad—*

130

Sindbad am I, sailor of Ocean,
Sailor of all of the Orient Seas

. . . ah yes, my fine young poet, you who do not even believe that I am telling the truth . . . at his hour, *Bibliac* is well more than a century ahead of us all, puzzling its way through the odd and cryptic works that will bejewel the distant future . . . don't you see, you young fool . . . *Bibliac will run forever,* tireless as any giant machine, filling its endless paper spools with the triumphs of literature from the thirtieth, the fortieth and even the fiftieth centuries . . . *to the last syllable of recorded time!"*

*

YOU ARE looking at me, young man, with very much the same sort of expression I must have worn, when the Gentleman in Green uttered those astounding words to me, decades ago. I have no doubt he was irritated by my vapid stare, my idiotic comments, my not-very-well-concealed air of ironic tolerance of what may, after all, have been the utterances of a madman, and not a mechanical genius whose subtle invention had riffled through the library-shelves of unborn Tomorrow.

What? Oh yes: what happened next. There is very little left to tell. He sprang up from the table in a spurt of anger—darted into the street—and was struck down by a bicyclist. His brow collided with the curbstone, splattering it with crimson . . . ah, I do not like to recall it, even now!

Hmm? Dead? Perhaps—I never knew. The crowd gathered swiftly, like human vultures drawn to the bright evidence of mortality. The *gendarmes* . . . the ambulance . . . I was shaken to the core of my spirit, and hesitated—a fatal hesitation—then he was gone, taken away to some unknown morgue or hospital, and my one and only chance to investigate the truth of his astounding claims, gone with him. You see, his name —his address—I never knew. Whether he lived or died —forever unknown to me.

But his memory has tortured me ever since. *Was* he just a clever cadger-of-drinks, who repaid the generous with a fine-spun romance? *Was* he just a cafe hanger-on, seeking the ear of the well-pursed, gullible tourist? Was he insane—deluded—a dreamer—an eccentric would-be inventor, seeking funds to finance some wild invention that would never see the light of day?

Or was he what he said, and all of his story sober truth?

Perhaps my first theory is the soundest of all. Surely, you, a journalist, must have listened to many surprising revelations over a free glass of liquor? I recall a grizzled Irishman for whom I once purchased a mug of good beer at McSorley's in New York; he confided hoarsely to me, in words breathed in a redolence of fermented malt, that he had sold his immortal soul to Asmodeus for eternal youth . . . but unfortunately had neglected to realize that eternal poverty went with the gift, since no conceivable amount of funds could support a man never to die! And then there was the bogus Italian count I met on the Riviera—twenty years ago, as I recall—who sponged a full week off a wealthy, occult-minded dowager, on the strength of his claim to be a genuine werewolf . . .

he left our mutual host before the full moon, and I have always rather regretted missing the test of his tale.

Alcohol will frequently bring out, even in the most common man,—the unexpected.

No, no, of course, you cannot publish this. Just write that I regret Pound died before getting his Nobel . . . or never having met Yeats. Or say something about how much I deplore the shape toward which modern literature is tending. Or anything you will. It hardly matters.

. . . But, if you will, remember those names. Paxton, Chiminez, de Montaubon, Jones, Von Bremen, Sir Edward Marlinson, Tierney. You are very young—scarce older than I when I met my Gentleman in Green; perhaps you will live long enough to see the appearance of *Those Who Err* . . . Ah, great God, but I envy you! *You will live to learn whether it was all true or not* . . . no, no. You must forgive me. Tears come easy to the old.

Yes, the river does look lovely from here. You should see it in June, with the willows dipping their thin green fingers in the shallows, against the rich curve of the cliffs beyond. On clear days, you can actually . . .

Ah. That must be my housekeeper; I expect it is time for your train. Thank you so much for stopping by. And—please—forgive an old man for rambling on so. There are so very few herabouts, with whom I can talk on intelligent topics. Yes, yes, certainly: just say I salute the memory of Pound, and regret having missed Yeats. Anything you like. Anything.

It doesn't really matter.

＊

＊

THE HEROIC FANTASY—the tale of quest or war or adventure, laid in an imaginary, pre-Industrial world of the author's own invention, a world where magic works and the Gods are real—was established by three unusual writers. The first of these was an eccentric English gentleman named William Morris (1834-1896) who literally founded the genre with such novels as *The Wood Beyond the World* (1895) and *The Well at the World's End* (1896); these are sprawling and immense novels of strange adventure in a dim, Medieval worldscape. (And when I say immense, I mean immense—*Well* is every inch of a quarter of a million words long.)

After Morris, came that extraordinary Anglo-Irish peer, Lord Dunsany (1878-1958), eighteenth in a line that has been called one of the most ancient baronial titles in the British Isles. If Morris was the first to explore the possibilities of the invented world, Dunsany was surely the second, although he worked more in the field of the short story than the epic-length novel. And following Dunsany, came the third of this trio: E. R. Eddison (1882-1945), who wrote that incredible masterpiece, *The Worm Ouroboros* (1922), and the three extraordinary, enduring and yet difficult books which form his Zimiamvia Trilogy.

From these three literary pioneers, descended all

134

the host of imaginative writers who have worked in this rich, ore-laden vein after them, a list which includes Robert E. Howard, Clark Ashton Smith, C. S. Lewis, H. P. Lovecraft, Fritz Leiber, James Branch Cabell, Fletcher Pratt, Poul Anderson, J. R. R. Tolkien, L. Sprague de Camp, John Jakes and Michael Moorcock.

And Lin Carter. For—all impertinent questions of "quality" set aside—I have for some time been working in this genre; to be precise, besides my familiar sword & sorcery stuff, I have for some ten or a dozen years (off and on) been puttering away at a titanic fantasy novel of amazing proportions which is completely in the Morris/Eddison/Tolkien tradition. If ever it is completed and published, it will be known as *Khymyrium: The City of the Hundred Kings, from the Coming of Aviathar the Lion to the Passing of Spheridion the Doomed*. In its final form, it will be about half again as massive as *The Lord of the Rings:* I only hope I can make it half as *good!*

For this last place in the book, it seems fitting to include something from the future, something still in the works, something not yet finished, hence I have included a tale from the first book of my *Khymyrium*.

The scene is this: a wandering young knight named Aviathar has come over into the Kingdom of Sarthay and guests for the night with Lord Gondomir, before continuing on his journey to the tournament of arms at Fontavery Downs. After dinner, Gondomir, Aviathar, and two other guests fall into conversation and therein somewhat of the background of the main story emerges. These other guests are a grim war-captain, Lynxias of Phome, who takes an instant and in-

135

stinctive dislike to the youth, Aviathar, and a small, quick-eyed, birdlike little augur, Chelian of Thax.

I selected this particular excerpt because it gives you a fairly good idea of the general flavor, color, mood and style of the novel-sequence in its entirety. . . .

THE MANTICHORE

From a Work-in-Progress

4. THEY JOIN IN A
ROUND OF CONVERSE

When that they were done and risen from their
meat, serfs who bore clasped about their necks collars
of thin silver cut with the Ram of Glasgerd drew up
great chairs before the roaring hearth for the Lord
Gondomir and the guests, and served them a night-
cup of hot mulled spice wine against the fever.

And the Lord Gondomir decreed a Round of Converse. Now this was a custom of olden-time among
the Children of Thlunlarna, from whose loins their
ancestors were sprung in Time Gone By; that each in
turn produce a topic of conversation, and the first
subject of the Round was proposed by the Lord
Lynxias, who spoke of war.

He recounted the tale of a campaign in which he
had but recent-served under that mighty warrior of
high renown, even the grim and warlike Zar of
Khadys, of whom it wast said, he fought more terribly

137

with his one strong hand than most men fight with their two.

This war had been foughten south of the Sea in those realms that lie huddled against the marches of the Land of Wizards below Tharsha. This was that time, now seven years agone, when the hosts of the Aophim had gone up against Sholgonda of the Waste, for that the Sholgondyana had long-harried their borders, bearing off their women to vile slavery, burning the farms on their marches, and seizing the heavy-laden caravans that do cross the Waste bound for the kingly cities to the East.

In blunt, terse phrases, all spiced and intermixed with weird and grisly oaths, the Lord Lynxias told of this venture, of its seiges, quarrels, expeditions, on-slaughts, forays, and pitch-battles, and it was a splendid tale he told, filled with mighty deeds and grim deaths and furious battlings, and the beautiful fall of heroes, while the youth, Avlathar, sat dreaming with remote eyes fixed on the flickering fire. He felt uncomfortable and out-of-place among so noble and high-born and far-traveled a company, for worldly and glittering lords such as these had ventured but seldom into hilly and transmarine Memnos where he had been born. Yet, withal, his hot blood sang to the high and daring deeds of which the Lord Lynxias made relation, and he fell adreaming of Sholgonda amid the Waste, that fair and immemorial city of red marble and black stone men call The Dream of the Desert, for that it doth arise within the sandy and mysterious Waste some say was made by the magic of the gnarly-folk in olden-time, who had first raised that city and who cursed it with a mighty curse what time, in their war with the Northlandermen who had come

138

reaving down from remote Torcys and Vodsmyr, they fell back in the last days of that immortal war and were not broken in battle, but withdrew from what had become the Lands of Men unto the very brink and edge of the world. And others said, and mayhap spoke in sooth, that it was the great hand of Dzimdzoul, the Wizard of the World, that fosterling and eldest child of the Gods, who didst lay the Curse of the Waste upon the fields about scarlet and black Sholgonda for the chastisement of dark and terrible Thathmool Kandathma, who of old did rule therein on a throne hewn from the heart of a single and gigantic ruby. Yet fair and famous was garden-girt Sholgonda, whose mighty and sunset-colored ramparts of sheer stone rose in a steep wall, lifting out of the very midst of the sea of sand, and the desert laps up against it as do the waves of the blue sea break against the high, up-rearing and embastioned front of some vast sea-affronting cliff.

Stirred by the tale of this war, in which the barren and impenetrable Waste alone had broken the host of the warlike Aophim, the Lord Gondomir thundered forth tales of ancient battles in the wars of his youth, what time the Twelve Barons of Sarthay had summoned the levy of the Shaws and the Dales and had gone up against the black city of Zarthex far to the west, in that cruel and barbaric land of heathenry where men still worship Nux the Demon of Old Night in curious and squeamish-making ways better left untold. And he spoke on half-forgotten campaigns and well-nigh legendary wars against those queer old towns tucked away amidst the folds of the grey hills, half-hidden as a woman hides her gemmy gauds among the tucks and gathers of her robes. They spoke of fabled, dim, remote Zekundemar deep in the Land of Wizards below savage Tharsha and beyond the green salt sea to the south, and of strange and awful battles filled with marvels and with thunderbolts, by which the Wizards broke forever the iron walls of evil Mandrakor. And young Aviathar, who had heard weird tales of this old war between the desert chiefs of Tharsha and the wizard-warriors of the Kingdom of Mystery, and had wondered thereat over the whispered rumors of this conflict, listened and dreamed of high deeds on the thundering plains of war.

And it came about that the Round of Converse passed to the Lord Gondomir, and he spoke of sport, of the hunt and the chase. And he told of his deeds that time, when, rousing the hounds and engathering about him the stout huntsmen and archers of Sarthay, he rode forth into the Hills of Thald to bring at last to bay before his steel that great Blue Boar of Tirith Palma, which long and long had ravaged the forest realm and was the scourge of all the farms and fields hereabouts. He told how that they did track the spoor three nights and three days down the Hills and down the river Silvernwater and past the Nool and deep and deeper than had ever huntsman gone before into that dark and dread forest called The Yethlerian Forest, whereof was far the greater part of all Sarthay encumbered.

And at the very last, deep in the twilit glades of the immemorial wild at the gloaming of the fourth day of the hunt, did they bring to bay this boar at last, coming up against a wall of impenetrable and interwoven thorn . . . and found there a gigantical and dreaded beast, even the fabulous and mighty Chirophanx, whose like had not been glimpsed within the Lands

140

of Men for seven generations of mortal memory, and who was perchance the very last of her enchanted and unearthly breed still dwelling in mortal fields. This fearsome and savage monster had come upon the Blue Boar ere ever they did come, and lo! it dangled from her incredible jaws. In a low voice, the lord told how they sat still as death, gripping their stallions between their knees with eyes fixed upon the sight of the awful Thing, which was after the likeness of a lion, but seventeen times the size of any lion ever glimpsed by men, and with eagle-wings so vast they could enshade the sky of noon, and (this was the most terrible of all) with the stupendous face of a woman set amidst the shaggy mane of a lion. It crunched and mangled the dead boar between unbelievable jaws, turning against them all the while great moon-eyes that blazed like globes of greenish phosphor-fire through the dimness of the ensorcelled dusk; and still they sat unmoving, without speech, in a chill sweat of horror, till at length it turned away and padded from the clearing upon ponderous paws that shook the earth a little beneath its enormous tread, bearing away the great boar dangling from blood-bedrabbled jaws as might some house-cat carry off a captured mouse, the which to devour at leisure and in privacy.

5. OF DARKLING AND OMINOUS THINGS

They were silent some little time after the Lord Gondomir had done with his relation, each in his own way ruminating on this amazing marvel. And then the Converse turned to matters spiritual, and the Abbot

Chelian made his contribution to the Round. As His Purity wore the Purple of Augury, the Lord Lynxias in a lazy and drawling voice made inquiry of those future things as yet deep-hidden in the womb of time unborn. He asked of war, and inquired perchance too boldly into the Abbot's mission unto the Oracle of the Speaking Stone at Islarch Keroona.

There was some hint of unease in the Augur's reply, and his words savored somewhat of the evasive in their import. His bearing seemed nervous; he fidgeted about in his chair; his alert, inquisitive eyes were veiled and hooded behind drooping lids.

"Well know we all," the Lord Lynxias was saying in his leisurely and round about way, one brown hand toying with the goblet, hot eyes roving restlessly about the hall filled now with gigantic velvet shadows, "that in Their good and due time the divine Taosar reveal that which They do desire that we shouldst know . . . as did the Red Sibyl foretell of the war betwixt the Aophim and the red city of Sholgonda, and how that the host under the great captaincy even of Zar of the One Hand should fail in this endeavor of arms, although one day yet still to come (unless I misremember me her prophecy) shall see my lord Zar bring down the pride of The Dream of the Desert, for thus is he destined to do, and lift up a strange new banner to fly from her black and crimson spires . . ."—and then, amidst all of this lazy meandering of speech, as was his way, the Lord Lynxias pounced without warning— ". . . and is *war* the matter over which Your Purity ventures south to the famous Oracle?"

Caught off balance by the sudden shrewdity of this unexpectedly direct query, the Abbot jumped and made a flickering of white hands, as it were, pushing away.

"I . . . no—no, indeed, Twice-Valiant . . . or at least I—I *think* not," he made a faltering reply.

Lynxias elevated one brow, sardonically, and smiled his cold, catlike, playful smile. He seemed to be baiting, even taunting, the small old priest, and he seemed to be enjoying it. Aviathar bethought him of how some men take curious, epicene pleasure in provoking and in teasing a weaker-than-they, incapable of striking back.

" 'No'—so positive!—and then, 'I think not'—less sure—" the war-captain smiled, toying with his cup. "In all honor, my lord Abbot, which is it?"

Flustered, the Augur said: "I . . . well, then, let me attempt explanation. Mine Brotherhood, you know, my lords, doth consist of Seers according to the various thirty-two disciplines of divination, as the Readers of the Planets, for example, or the Interpreters of Dreams, or the Alectromancers, and suchlike. In general course, we may, by our mastery of the requisite skills, and always under dependency to the favor of Taos Sarganastor our Lord and Patron, read aright the signs of the futurity as they are figured forth in this or that aspect of Nature, many-faced and multiform, which emblems and signals are spelled out in the lore-books of our Science. But . . . of late, there have been . . . certain . . . *signs* . . ."

The Abbot left the single word hanging there in the smoky air. Gondomir blinked.

"Aye?" he prompted. "Signs?"

The Augur released a troubled sigh. "Aye, my lord. Certain—portents. Omens. That have been observed. And certain devout and gifted Seers have been visited

143

with disturbing and ambiguous dreams, curiously defiant of interpretation by all traditional and holy methods. And add unto this sum, the matter of the ever-moving stars of heaven . . . for the celestial orbs are even now as I speak, assembling into an ominous and unsettling configuration . . ."

He broke off, as if his mind wandered from the pattern of his speech into some private pathway. Then: "Why, I, even I, on the road hither from my abbey in the town of Thax didst behold a Bearded Star go rushing past above my head through the dim empurpled night with all its whispers and its silences . . . it went hissed and spluttering down the vault of eternal heaven and through the blue and bottomless sky of evening . . . and, as the gloaming deepened into dusk and thence into the dark of night, and the stars like flowers on a summer field, opened one by one in spheres of softly golden light above the darkling lands wherethrough I passed . . . I, to my horror (as you may conjecture) saw that these everlasting orbs were set-awry from their accustomed coign, all subtly out-of-place, as dislodged from their sphere by some supernal and omnific Hand, and all the night around me was quick with fiery signs and portents marvelous and strange . . . and suchlike, good my lords, and, aye, even those matters strangelier than these . . ."

His tones quavered away into hushed, uneasy silence, and the others glanced each to each with eyes that shone fearfully in the reflex of the fire-blaze.

At length the Lord Lynxias again spoke, promptingly, goading the reluctant Abbot into further speech.

"Somewhat I know of the Starry Science," he observed coolly. "What other matters even strangelier than these do you think on? And signs—specifically?"

A bit irritably, the Abbot roused himself and shot a glance tinged of some slight malice at the coolly spoken war-captain and his mocking half-smile.

"The Bale Star sits in the Constellation of the Seventh Basilisk," Chelian said with sharp, precise words, each bitten off with thinned lips set in a chill, small smile of cold reproof. "The red spark of Shombareen hath been observed rising into the House of the Sphinx, and the green eye of Oropus smoulders at the heart of The Vortex. High in the eastern sky over the Maremma, the Sword of Stars is in the ascendent . . . for the first time within the memory of man. And that great and portentious star that we call Zarizel the White sits at the apex of the House of the Green Lion, where from of old hath sat the famous star Bel-Manderzool!"

Such things were unheard-of—terrifying! They drew in their breath sharply, and Lynxias narrowed his eyes a little, blinking warily, again like some great cat.

"Strange . . . and strange, in very sooth!" he said thoughtfully, a little in awe, and there was now no token or trace of provokingness or mockery in his tones. "And the Planets—what of them?" he asked.

The little Abbot huddled in the swathings of his mulberry-purple robes, and his face was as a fleshless white mask, stark and hysteric in the half-dark, half-light of the enshadowed room, about whose walls the storm shrieked and bellowed with wind and lashing rain and trumpet-throated thunders.

"They, too, shadow forth omens momentous, cryptic, baffling to the reading. For the greater Planets of

145

Anthedon and Golonessa, Kazibuth and crimson Phere, are approached nigh unto a rare and unusual conjunction, such as hath not been seen in these heavens for full one thousand years. And the lesser Planets, too, that are Ithome, Jasphar, and golden Phambelzoond, are lifting far beyond their eternal and familiar circuits into a difficult and terrible relationship which augurs . . . *we know not what.*" He sighed, and was silent for a spell.

Then: "Signs such as these . . . weird, unreadable, puzzling in the obscurity of their proximations . . . my lords, they bode not well, methinks, for these realms about us. Or," he clarified, in his precise, sharp way, "it is either that they bode a very great ill, or a very great good, the which we are not at all certain. Hence do I venture south of these lands unto the world-famous Oracle at Islarch Keroona. For these signs, in very truth, shadow forth dimly and in unsure fashion, a great and far-reaching change of thrones, perchance . . . some shifting in the balance of power, in these realms about the Two Rivers . . ."

6. WHEREIN THEY SPEAK OF THE WOMAN

Then, and unexpectedly, spake the Lord Gondomir.
"I have heard from a traveling bard in Thios-town that a new God hath yet to ascend from mortality into the Divine Sphere. Now, look you: might not an Apotheosis be so figured forth with fiery signs upon the face of heaven, and with sleep-disturbing dreams and visions vouchsafed unto those sworn to the holy life?"

Lynxias smiled—it was a coarse and vulpine leer—

and spat into the clean, dry rushes. "Bards! Shallow-witted fools, one and all, and not worthy the sweat it takes to slay them. Put no credence in suchlike babble, my lord baron!"

"Not so, Twice-Valiant!" the spry little Abbot twittered, seeming eager for this change in the direction of the discourse. "Now what sayeth the maxim? 'Tis . . . let me see . . . one of the last in Phodazlimar the Gray Book . . . I think me so. Ah!" And closing his eyes in thought, he chanted in a reedy voice:

> *Four occupations only*
> *Are fit for a man lifelong:*
> *War-faring, King-ship, God-priesting*
> *The Making of Song.*

Gondomir continued: "Nay, but truly! It was a deep saying, and the singer no spindle-shanked minstrel, but a hero-bard . . . a true Rhapsode, a master with both the sword of war and the lute of song."

"Ah, a Rhapsode! Then that is indeed another matter," conceded Lynxias.

Gondomir blinked into his wine-cup, ruminatively.

"This new God is to be a Divine Lady. The Rhapsode told they rumored it She hath but recent been born of a mortal woman at Shialmar in Phasia, or there-about . . ."

The Abbot set this matter aside with a brisk flutter of small white hands.

"True, true, all this is known, and is not the cause of the signs and portents—why, the Red Sibyl of Zokara hath ﹨proclaimed Her Incarnation this twelve-month-since; She is yet but a babe—"

The Lord Lynxias arched a brow, with a politely

sardonic smile. "Now, by the Bull of Vrain, but this is odd!" he laughed.

The Abbot Chelian looked a look of inquiry at him. "How so, my lord? How so 'odd'?"

"Why, if the Taosar seek a new Goddess, why raise Her amongst heathenish Zokara-folk, where Magicians are more in credit than are priests? And why seek over-sea for Her . . . when all the while, and right near at hand in the Maremma, as I have heard, dwelleth a Lady of Power nigh fit for Taos-Mountain? Aye! They need look no farther than across the Jander—eh?"

Gondomir turned a face of grim iron upon his guest.

"No more on this, Twice-Valiant. We do not discuss such matters here."

Lynxias smiled incredulously. "What? But—my lord —I do not—"

"*No.*" Gondomir's voice was flat and hard; even Aviathar blinked with surprise at the sudden note of command. "In this land—and in mine hall—decent folk avoid mention of *Her,* as do they keep tongue from naming that darkling realm wherein She queens it. 'The Dubious Land' they call it, here-abouts."

In his bantering, yet ingratiating way, Lynxias could not refrain from saying yet more. "Even as you say, my good lord, but—come! The honor of it!—To have a Goddess for a neighbor—!"

"*Enough!*" the baron shouted in a voice of thunder. There was a moment of shocked silence; Aviathar noticed that even bold Lynxias winced and shrank back. With an effort, the purple-faced old baron mastered his temper. Then, in a more quiet, controlled tone he said: "No Goddess, She, but a foul witch who work-

148

eth Her dark marvels on the land by means of demon-wrested lore, bought for I-know-not-what ungodly price, and grisly arts culled out of books of dark thaumaturgies that shouldst be given over to the purifying flames. Out of the shadowy-lands She came some ten years agone, and to the shadows She shall someday go—and none too soon for we folk of Sarthay. If that sounds strange and wondrous to your ears, think thee on this: in your most westerly and distant realm, my lord, you but hear echoes of marvels, and think them fair, as they touch upon you not. But there are those within an league of here, fled to Sarthay whose fathers from the older-times were Maremma-bred, couldst tell thee such tales as thou wouldst not dare sleep this night, for fear of dreaming! Aye. Here in the forest realm, we live almost beneath the shadow of Her hand, and we treat not such matters lightsomely. Thus: no more on this, as you are my guest and beholden to me for mine courtesy. Come, no more."

Lynxias' purring voice fell into unctuous and most conciliatory phrases: "With all my heart, good my Lord! I . . . I slip sometimes into a casual mode of speech and my tongue wags in ways my heart would have it not: it is an old fault. I intended not to be affrontive nor offend mine host, but—the lateness of the hour, and the vintage of your wine, perchance—led me unconsciously into areas of converse displeasing. Enough—let it be forgotten as you will!"

Gondomir nodded, courtequsly. "Forgotten it is, Twice-Valiant. We'll speak on it no more."

Lynxias stirred himself restlessly. "Come, come, now," he said, turning to silent Aviathar. "Let us guide the course of our Round into less troubled waters, as the Poet saith! Sir swordsman, here, who speaks so little but, I swear, observes all: is it not his turn to lead our Converse?"

The others loudly called upon the youth to propose the next topic. Aviathar, who by this late hour felt at his ease amongst the company, modestly yielded. The discomforts he had felt in so noble and worldly a company had ebbed, as well, due to the pleasures of a full belly, and the hot spiced wine to which a frugal upbringing had failed to accustom him to, perchance contributed to the unlocking of his tongue.

7.   AVIATHAR TELLETH HIS TALE

They drew from him at length his story. He was the younger of two sons born to an ancient Vodsmyrian house long-since fallen upon evil times and declined from former greatness into current obscurity, although he was resigned to this eclipse in the fortunes of his house and felt no bitterness at his spendthrift father, since dead of the rheum. In this context he quoted the maxim: "For each new oak that riseth to o'ertop the forest, one must fall to make the room for it," which the Abbot Chelian applauded as most apt.

His father's bleak, small keep amidst the Hills of Koriath, and what little lands were left under their Seal, all hadst gone to his elder brother as the heir. And thus had Aviathar, in the traditional ways of the younger son, ridden forth into the wide-wayed world astride a spavined nag to seek what rewards Fortune might reserve for the scion of a noble but impoverished line.

He had ventured first to Memnos, that old grey town beside the Hyzaspes, wherefrom once, in olden, golden time, had ridden forth out of the Leopard Gate under the shadow of a thousand rustling banners gallant Belnarth of the Spear, what time he went up against Lisimbra of the Seven Gates. But Aviathar had found therein no employment for his steel. They of Memnos-town were old and tired now, and long-since had forgot the high heroic days of Belnarth the Brave and the looting of seven-gated Lisimbra by the Sundering Seas. The bright, high-hearted glory of olden days had arisen up and gone forth out of old grey Memnos, where she lay girdled with time-ravaged and crumbling walls, dreaming her centuries away by the slow sliding silver floods of the Hyzaspes. They thought no more in olden Memnos of war and conquest and splendid treasure wrested by the strength of steel, nor sang the war-bards any longer in that town.

Thence had Aviathar gone over-river to the sister-city of Vrain, where of old the hero Asterion fetched from the halls of Pteraphon the Lord of Shadows that mighty man-tall Silver Bull for which the town hast ever been in song. And therein he took service with the Prince Elverus of Vrain, Seventh Of That Name. And then unto his audience did this Aviathar unfold a tale weird, curious and full of marvels, and nigh passing all belief.

This town of Vrain lay midway betwixt that range of mountains men call The Wall and the blue scimitar of the Sundering Sea. And from the slopes of that mighty row of mountains the green ranks of a vast army of trees marched down nigh unto the very walls of Vrain, as though the forest wouldst lay siege unto

151

the city, and this was known from of old as the Wood of the Well, for that marvel which lay deep in the midst of it, and therein dwelt many strange wonders that yet survived into the world from olden-time. Now when Aviathar was in the sixth month of his service unto the Prince of Vrain, from the heart of this marvelous wood had come up against the walls of the city an savage and ferocious monster called the Mantichore, most ill-shapen and horrible to the eye, formed after the likeness of a gigantical and blood-red lion, but thrice-and-more the size of any lion yet seen by eyes of men through all the eternal circuit of the ever-rolling years. It bore the face of a man, framed in its scarlet and leonine mane, and the jaws thereof had three rows of triangle-shapen fangs. The claws of the monster were all a-twisting and spiraled like unto a carpenter's screws, and it carried a long up-curving tail, thick-tufted with spiny bristles as en-venomed as the sting of scorpion or multipede.

This demon-begotten thing of nightmare didst prowl about the walls and beleaguer the city of Vrain, and slaughtered every warrior and champion the Prince Elverus dispatched against it, tearing both man and stallion apart and devouring their smoking bowels and entrails in full view of the townsfolk on the city walls, nor might any of the Five Weapons of War cause it aught of hurt or harm, for that its flesh and hide were of a hardness like unto red marble-stone. And the Prince and the people despaired, and wept and made much lamentation, bewailing that this cursed hell-spawned thing had come up against them, and they prayed unto the Most High Gods and offered sacrifice and beseeched the aid of the Taosar, yet naught betid and ever the great scarlet beast

152

prowled about the walls and went unslain of men or Immortals.

And one night it came to pass after this fashion, that the youth Aviathar, being housed with the other warriors in the barracks of the palace of the Prince, didst sleep and in this sleep there did come unto him a dream of miracles and it seemed there appeared before him, out of a roiling of sable smokes, the mighty form of a great warrior armed and clothed in the helm and hauberk of a hero, yet with the wing-adorned brow of Divinity. And in a voice like unto the song of a great and brazen trumpet of war, this phantasm named itself with 'the great name of the God Marmaranax the Lord of Ten Thousand Battles, and the God commanded the sleeping youth to rise up and seek for the mighty Sword of the Lion where it lay these thousands of uncounted years beneath the Hill of Skulls.

And all of this did the youth Aviathar perform, and that directly upon awakening in the first pale radiance of the dawn, and as this hill whereof the Lord of Battles spake, it lay some little ways beyond the city wall where in olden-times the lords of Vrain had made burial of their dead who wert slain in war against the gnarly-folk who had held all of this land of Cydace before the coming of mankind. And thus the youth went out of the city by a little door he knew of, but in great care and quiet for dread of the crimson beast, and came unto this hilly mound and dug therein, deep-delving in the hot loam, and lo! he didst uncover there a long and narrow tabernacle of purest shining brass wherein was laid a very great' sword of ancient and glorious work, and not fashioned by the hands of men, and the brand bore upon

153

the glittering mirror of its blade, on the one side, the legend: I AM AZLON THE GREAT, THE SWORD OF THE LION; and, on the other, this: DRAW ME IN NAUGHT BUT A JUST CAUSE; and at all of this he marveled exceeding, as he knelt there in the dewy earth of dawn.

As his audience sat enthralled at this strange tale, all save for the Lord Lynxias who wast unmoved and who smiled him a small and skeptical smile, this Aviathar told how all of a sudden had the Mantichore come upon him there as he was on his knees with the bright sword blazing in the grasp of his trembling hands.

Its white and glistening manlike visage hideous under the bristling spiky mane, its mad eyes glaring like meteors in the dark and mighty limbs carnation-crimson as a sunset sky, and a-lashing of its terrible and thorny tail, the thing gave voice to a harsh and clarion-throated scream of daemonic laughter that nigh to split the blue welkin as might a thunderclap, and it sprang upon him then. And ere he could move or think or even start in terror, the youth felt himself seized up in a thrilling rush of irresistible power that surged from the mighty swordhilt in his palm and sent an electric thrill of weird and terrifying strength seething through his every sinew and limb. And almost as with a volition of its own, his arm moved. The sword Azlon swept up, sun-flashing, in a glittering arc like that curve of green phosphoric fire the fallen star traces adown the midnight vault of heaven. The dazzling blade came whistling down even as the beast sprang and it cleft the agate-chested Mantichore in twain with an single stroke as it had been naught

154

but an empty shape cut from flimsy paper for a child's toy.

> And in this wise was Azlon the Great,
> the mightiest of all the Swords of Power
> upon the earth, wielded in war-faring
> again in the Lands of Men for the first
> time in an thousand centuries.

*

I stuck this one in, folks, because I thought you might like to see an excerpt from a current work-in-progress, together with all this other stuff, some of which dates back many years. If it happens you *did* like this excerpt, and would like to go on and read more of *Khymyrium* soon, well, you're out of luck. I've got ten or fifteen more years of work to put in on it before it will be ready. Sorry.

Worlds aren't built in a day, you know. Not worlds like Khymyrium's, anyhow!

*

A Few Last Words

SO THERE you have it, friends: a mixed bag of Carterana. A couple straight science fiction yarns, a science fiction parody, a morsel of science fiction humor, a short weird, a piece of classical-type Sword & Sorcery, an excerpt from a work-in-progress of the subgenre of epic fantasy. A comprehensive tour of the Lin Carter mind, with typewriter instead of gun and camera.

I enjoy whacking out yarns, but I have to admit I have more fun writing novels than short stories. Novels give you more leeway and latitude. You've got more room to swing your arms: more elbow-space. And I like the freedom to create whole *worlds* . . . to build them from the magma up, complete with maps, mythologies, feigned histories and brand spanking new Pantheons: the whole works. This sort of thing, well, it's the sort of thing you just can't do in short story lengths. With the exception of a series of short stories, of course.

But there's a certain element of fun to writing short stories, too. A brand of pleasure completely different from the sort of enjoyment I get from writing a novel. Short stories give you the chance to experiment with variations in style; you can pull off certain tricks and use certain narrative devices you can't very well use in the novel.

So I will probably keep right on writing both. And you may, unless the foregoing sample scares you away for good, yes, you may very well find yourself reading another collection of these things about this same time next year—who knows?

Let's see . . . that Simrana yarn I didn't get back from my agent in time to put in here . . . and there's that story I just sold to Ted White for *Fantastic*, "A Guide to the City" and that wacky time-travel yarn I keep forgetting about . . . and that horror tale Augie Derleth will be running in *The Arkham Sampler* later on this year . . . yeah!

See you next year, folks.

—LIN CARTER

❀